BID TIME RETURN

Recent Titles by Frances Paige from Severn House

THE CONFETTI BED
A DAY AT THE RACES
GAME TO MISS COWAN
LOVE IS A STRANGER
PASSIONS OF THE MIND
SO LONG AT THE FAIR
THE SUMMER FIELDS
THE SWIMMING POOL

BID TIME RETURN

Frances Paige

This first world edition published in Great Britain 2003 by
SEVERN HOUSE PUBLISHERS LTD of
9–15 High Street, Sutton, Surrey SM1 1DF.
This first world edition published in the USA 2003 by
SEVERN HOUSE PUBLISHERS INC of
595 Madison Avenue, New York, N.Y. 10022.

British Library Cataloguing in Publication Data

Paige, Frances
  Bid time return
  1. Young women - Scotland - Glasgow - History - 20th century
      - Fiction
  2. Bereavement - Fiction
  3. Glasgow (Scotland) - Social life and customs - 20th century
      - Fiction
  I. Title
  823.9'14 [F]

ISBN 0-7278-6006-2

Typeset by Hewer Text Ltd.,
Edinburgh, Scotland.
Printed and bound in Great Britain by
MPG Books Ltd., Bodmin, Cornwall.

To Simon

One

When Jane Mackie's father died at forty-five of a heart attack, she realized later that she had lost a friend as well. It was he who had encouraged her to think of going to university, like Robert, her brother. Her mother had tacitly given into the idea, but when James Mackie's affairs were cleared up, she told Jane there was no longer any chance of university. Robert was getting a grant from Carnegie. There was no possibility that Jane would be given one, judging by her school results. That great benefactor of Glasgow, Sir Andrew Carnegie, had been dedicated to helping only bright pupils. The best thing for her to do was to put the idea out of her head, and concentrate on going to a business college. Jane felt that it gave her mother a certain satisfaction in saying this. She didn't believe in girls having a 'good' education, except what they gained from their mothers.

Then God help me! shouted Jane's inner voice, which she used to keep herself sane.

A pall seemed to fall over the house when Robert went off to university. With the death of her husband, her mother looked to Jane for company, but they had nothing in common. Margaret Mackie's interests lay in housekeeping, and the hope that her daughter would find, as she put it, 'a good man'. On the other hand, her father had discussed world affairs and politics with her. He had taken her to the theatre, particularly the Citizens Theatre in Glasgow, well-known for its avant-garde plays; had discussed her set reading at school with her: Aldous Huxley, Virginia Woolf; and on rare occasions, when an opera company visited Glasgow, they went together. Margaret Mackie, when invited to accompany them, said it was all 'above her head'. Which was true enough, Jane realized. Only later in her life had she realized how inadequate her mother must have felt compared with her husband.

She knew her mother had been a farmer's daughter, and she and her father had met by chance. He had been studying architecture, and taking part in a dig in her village. He and his fellow students had gone to the local dance at the village hall where he had met Margaret, and it had been a case of love at first sight.

Jane and Robert, when they were together, often discussed their parents, and had agreed that their marriage was an awful warning to them. Their parents had been unsuited to each other, they both agreed, having been witnesses to their constant quarrelling. You have to feel sorry for her, Robert often said, she's disadvantaged, not realizing that the word could apply to him and Jane. Neither of them took into account what their mother could have given them, had she not been so overawed by her husband. She had a natural affinity with nature and its lore, could grow plants, and understand them, but as they lived in a flat in the city and didn't have a garden, she never got the chance to demonstrate her gifts. She had many skills she could have imparted to Jane, but had no gift as a teacher, because of her short temper. She had always felt inferior to her husband, and when Robert and

Jane grew up, and became part of the family, she felt she was outnumbered. Her frustration showed itself in her sudden rages, which the whole family had to suffer.

Jane had confided to Robert, 'She's always advising me to "take a cat of my own kind", when choosing a husband, but she doesn't realize she should have taken that advice herself.'

'Perhaps we don't realize the power of love,' Robert had joked. Neither of them had ever been gripped by passion, like their parents. Like most young people they thought they knew all the answers.

The next bombshell to drop on the household after James' death came in a letter from Robert to his mother. 'Look at this!' Margaret Mackie threw it across the table to Jane.

'Is it from Robert?' she said, recognizing the hand-writing.

'Yes, and don't tell me you didn't know about this. You two are as thick as thieves.'

Jane quickly scanned the letter: 'I'm dropping out, Mother. I don't find anything of interest here for me. I've been offered a job on a sheep farm near Auckland in New Zealand by the father of a lad whom I've met here, and I've decided to take it. I must have inherited the farming instinct from you.'

Robert, trying to be light-hearted, she thought. She also felt slightly annoyed that he hadn't confided in her, but recognized he had their mother's ability to make quick decisions. Indeed, she thought, now with this farming idea, he was more like her than he realized.

1942

It was now eight years since James Mackie had died, and

Robert was doing well in New Zealand, judging by the happy letters he sent home. Jane was a personal assistant to the director of a large engineering firm, and she and her mother had settled down together in some sort of amity. Jane had learned to be careful of her mother's temper, and to keep her own counsel. She often thought it was like an armed truce, but her suggestion that she move into a flat of her own was greeted with anger and tears. She felt cornered.

This particular evening Jane was standing looking out of the window of their flat in Jordanhill, a suburb of Glasgow's west end. 'Eight p.m.,' Elma, her friend, had said. 'When you see the taxi, run downstairs. It will save me getting out. Be sure and be ready.' How like Elma, Jane thought. Full of plans which never quite worked out. Ten past, and no sign of them yet.

'I thought you said they were coming at eight o'clock,' her mother said from her seat at the fire. The familiar carping tone, Jane thought. Not all widows were like her. Look at Elma's mother . . .

'That's what Elma said.'

'To think of the trouble I had with that green lace, and how the draping at the back was that difficult to make it hang right . . .'

Who asked you to? Privately Jane had thought the draping looked like wings on either side of the low back of the dress she was wearing, but she hadn't dared make any comment, since her mother, pleased that she was going to a dance at the university, had made the dress for her.

Here was a car, no, it was that young man in the main-door flat who had bought a car recently, to the delight of his wife, and who was now one up on all her neighbours. '*We're going for a run down the coast in our car*,' was her

4

familiar boast. Yes, it was George Paterson. There was Betty welcoming him at the door.

'It said eight thirty on the ticket Elma gave you, didn't it? You'll never be there on time. Funny you should have to buy your own ticket.'

'Medical students don't have much money. You couldn't expect them to *pay* for our tickets.' Elma's boyfriend, Bob Sharp, had been the instigator of the outing. He had a friend, John Maxwell, a medical student, who had got tickets for the dance in the university, and Bob had suggested the foursome. Elma had had trouble persuading Jane, who didn't like the idea of a blind date, to make up the foursome for the hop.

To Jane's consternation, her mother had bought the green lace material for her dress at Copland & Lye's where 'she just happened to be'. She couldn't resist it, she had said, it was such a bargain, and she had 'just happened to see' a Butterick pattern which had actually suggested lace as the material. Jane, knowing how her mother liked planning dresses and stitching them on her Singer, didn't recognize this as creativity, but hadn't protested, knowing that if she did it would cause a row. Not for the first time she envied Robert, safe in Auckland, thus escaping his mother's dominance and fulfilling his longing for wide open spaces in one fell swoop. He had done well, to the extent of marrying the farmer's daughter, Meg, his friend's sister, thus establishing himself as an icon in his family: 'Look how well your brother has done!'

'In my young days men didn't keep girls waiting . . . Yes, the green lace drapes at the back very nicely . . .'

Jane saw a black taxi creeping along Clarence Drive, hesitantly. It must be it. It was! It had stopped at the entry, and she heard the toot of the horn.

'This is me!' she said, lifting her silver handbag and the shawl lying on the couch beside her. 'I've got my keys. I'll try not to be too late. I expect it will go on till one o'clock, though . . .' She turned and looked at her mother sitting disconsolately at the fire. Poor soul, but I wouldn't have given up lightly the chance of going to a dance at the university. 'I'm away then, Mother.' She waited for the words she always hoped for: 'Have a good time, dear', but they never came, and sighing inwardly, she made for the door. 'Ask Mrs Brown to come in and have a cup of tea with you.' she said, putting her hand on her mother's shoulder as she passed, but her answer was to shrug off the hand. Jane opened the door, went through the dark hall and seizing the handle of the main door of the flat, went out, resisting the desire to bang it behind her.

A young man was standing outside the taxi. 'I'm John Maxwell,' he said. 'Jump in at the front.' He opened the door.

'Right.' She got into the taxi.

He came in after her. 'Hope you won't be crushed,' he said.

Elma spoke from the back, 'We're a bit late, Jane. It was their fault. They were late in coming.'

'We're very sorry,' John Maxwell said. His voice was deep, and seemed to reverberate in the taxi. The driver muttered something about the traffic. Jane glanced sideways at the young man who was to be her partner for the evening. She had an impression of dark eyes, dark curly hair and a smile. How would he see her? Red-gold hair, set off by the green lace (Mother wasn't daft), the wings hidden by the Indian shawl with the silk fringe, which she had been allowed to choose for her twenty-first birthday, three years ago. Her mother had paid. The assistant in the shop had said it came from Srinagar, which had seemed a magical word to Jane at the time.

'I'm crushing you,' he said, and put his arm round her.

'It didn't matter to me,' Jane said in reply to Elma, 'but you know my mother.'

'Mrs Mackie's very particular,' Elma said, and laughed. 'Don't, Bob! But she is, isn't she, Jane?'

'I suppose so. Not like your mother.' Mrs Craig enjoyed Elma's friends coming to their house. Compared to her mother, Jane thought she was too flirty with them, but at least she made them welcome. She often wished her mother could be as free and easy as Elma's.

Respect for authority, whichever guise that was dressed in, be it for parents, teachers, policemen, or doctors, was the tenet by which Jane's mother had always lived. It made for a cheerless household.

Once at the dance hall, Jane was able to look properly at John Maxwell, and liked what she saw. His brown eyes, full of laughter, rested appreciatively on her, and she was instantly and completely and hopelessly in love. At least that was what it felt like as she was bewitched by his whole persona, his ready laughter. They danced together all evening, which suited Elma and Bob, who did the same. Once, when the two couples whirled past each other, John called, 'Look, you two, I've got an angel with green wings!' You're vindicated, Mother, Jane's inner voice said.

She had never known such a sense of relief, that she was free of her mother's forbidding presence, that the dress was all right, that she liked her partner, and his hand on her bare back. During a waltz, she was surprised to find that she had put her head on his shoulder, and

7

that he had wrapped his arms round her. At last, she thought, I've met someone who appeals to me, and whom I can escape with. She lifted her head and met his eyes, and she thought, He feels the same. We're in love. It's a new life for me.

The confirmation, that there was a world out there where, in spite of the gloominess of the war and her home background, she could find such enjoyment with John, such rib-aching hilariousness, grew during the evening. With each burst of laughter, her mother's precepts fell by the wayside. Life, she discovered, could be fun. Elma had been telling her that for ages. 'Your mother's sorry for herself. That's what's wrong with her. You have to go out and find happiness for yourself.'

John, fortunately, who had always been aware of this fun (his upbringing had been entirely different), felt that Jane was the girl he would like to spend the rest of his life with. He had never known anyone with such a sweetly solemn face which so easily could be made to dissolve into laughter at his quips. He saw the pale cheeks become rosily pink, the shy appreciation, her wide eyes narrowing and screwing up with laughter at his teasing. And when he commented on the beauty of those eyes, she looked so astonished and grateful that he felt ten feet tall. He was hooked for life.

John and Jane. We shall be one, they both agreed, but unfortunately ran against opposition from Jane's mother. Although she had always urged Jane to find 'a good man', now that she had apparently done this, Margaret Mackie was full of objections. John hadn't a job. Besides, he was liable to be called up. Instead of setting up a home, she suggested that they would be better to move in with her. Jane was horrified at this idea,

8

as John was, and said so. 'She's trying to hold on to you,' he said.

The next part of the 'campaign' as John called it, was Jane wakening to sounds of weeping from her mother's room, and once, she woke up to find her mother standing at her bedside, staring down at her. She had left the room without speaking. Jane lay shaking, admitting to herself that there was something about her mother's behaviour which frightened her. 'It was scary,' she told John.

'She's crazy,' he replied. He had told his parents, and his mother, who couldn't imagine that anyone would object to her son, had offered to call on Mrs Mackie. Privately, his father had advised him to look elsewhere.

The visit was a failure. Her mother wouldn't talk about it to Jane, but Mrs Maxwell said to her husband that she was an odd woman, quite unapproachable, fussed about the tea she had prepared, as if it mattered. 'They're very much in love,' Mrs Maxwell had said to her. 'Remember how we both felt when we were young, Mrs Mackie . . .'

'But she looked at me as if I were mad,' she later told her husband, 'and said it wouldn't last.'

'John should find someone else,' he had said, reiterating his opinion.

But what Mr Maxwell didn't know was that Jane was her father's daughter. She knew her mother's intimidating presence, and the effect it would have on Mrs Maxwell. Her mother would not have been able to tell Mrs Maxwell that she couldn't bear the thought of losing her daughter, because she had no resources of her own. Jane's role, as designated by her, was to protect her from the world, as her husband had done.

Jane agreed to marry John at a registry office, and then

present it as a fait accompli to her mother, and this they did. He couldn't understand her mother, nor her tight-lipped silence, but Jane realized that those who have never been in close contact with someone who is de-ranged are unable to imagine the atmosphere they create. It was to be a salutory lesson in John's career.

'I've got to get a job,' John said. His studies were over, he had successfully passed his examinations and was now a fully-fledged doctor. 'Don't worry, darling. I'll take care of you,' he said.

'First, we'll go to Fife to visit my Aunt Mary,' Jane said. 'She's asked us to spend our honeymoon at her farm.'

'I've never heard of her before.'

'I think she and Mother quarrelled, but I had this nice letter from her saying that she would be glad if we came to The Neuk, that's the name of the farm.'

'Great! Anything that saves us money is welcome.' He also thought that it would be a good idea to get Jane out of Glasgow and as far away from her mother as possible.

The farm was situated in a little village near Cupar, and they received a warm welcome from Aunt Mary and Uncle Joe. The house was large, and they were intrigued with the huge kitchen where Molly, the maid, spent two hours every day pumping water for the household sup-ply. It was the hub of the house.

Their two sons, Rab and Iain, and Molly sat down to eat with them, and John got on well with the sons, who teased him unmercifully about getting himself spliced. They were in no hurry, they said. Molly had a beau, Fraser, and he sometimes joined them at the table, and the company, so relaxed compared with Jane's home life, was a joy to her, as was the huge bed, with its cold linen sheets, allotted to them. Between them, they cuddled the stone hot-water bottle which Molly filled for them each night.

One evening, when John had gone to the pub with the boys, Jane was alone with her aunt. 'I'm glad of the chance to speak to you, Aunt,' she said. 'My mother was opposed to me getting married, and I had to make a choice. John has no idea what it was like living with her, and I've not talked about it to him.'

'Yes, I can see he's an easy-going lad, and from a good home, but don't keep any secrets from him. Tell him how difficult it's been for you. You two will be happy, I can see that.'

'Could you tell me something about my mother, what she was like at home? She came to depend on me when my father died, and Robert's been away. At first she gave me the impression that she wanted me to be married, but when John came on the scene, she resented him.'

'Margaret's always been hard to understand. Well, I'll tell you about her background, and maybe it will be a clue to what she's like now. She was the youngest of the family. Spoiled by us older ones, and then when our mother died, she was spoiled by our father. He indulged her in every possible way. Deterred suitors, and there were plenty, because she was a fine-looking girl, wheat-coloured hair, rosy cheeks, but a defiant manner which made her disliked by many in the village. She treated the workers in and around the farm in an autocratic way, and teased the young men who came for the hay-making. She had a terrible temper, and woe betide anyone who crossed her. Father let her get away with murder, and she was disliked by the women in the village because she broke so many hearts.

11

'But when your father came along, Father couldn't stand him. Didn't like his city ways, and tried to turn Margaret against him. The rows that went on in the house were terrible . . . they didn't care who was watching, and I know I often felt ashamed of her behaviour. But it was no good trying to remonstrate with her. She was wilful. She started slipping out to meet James, and then when he went back to Glasgow, she took the train there to meet him. He didn't get a chance to resist her. Then she became pregnant . . .' She stopped. 'Maybe you didn't know that?'

'No. I didn't. You mean . . . Robert?'

Her aunt nodded. 'There was a terrible row in the house, with an audience as usual. The boys had to restrain Father. "Try and stop me now!" she shouted at him, and he struck her across the face. The boys jumped on him, and held him off her, and I took her away to our room, where she behaved like someone who had taken leave of her senses. You can see me, Jane, I'm calm, I don't lose my temper, and I couldn't deal with her at all.'

'So, did her father give in to them marrying?'

'Had to. There was a hurried marriage, and James' family came and everyone tried to make it a happy day. She looked beautiful, and James was so fond of her, but I felt she was to blame for the baby . . . What am I saying? But from the first I thought they were ill-suited.'

'They quarrelled a lot, but Father was quiet.'

'I'm going to say something to you, Jane, which may distress you, but you don't look as if you've taken after her, either in looks or temperament. Once Dr Nesbitt said to me when I met him in the village . . . well, he stopped his pony and trap, I can see him now leaning down to me and saying, "Jump in, Mary, I want to have a chat with you . . ." And I did. He asked how your mother was getting on, and I told him that she was living in Glasgow with James. Of course, he knew she was married, and expecting, and he said she had come to see him because she wondered why her stomach was swelling! When he expressed surprise at her not admitting to know, she had flown into a rage, and he had to calm her down before he could let her leave the surgery. "I'm afraid that young man she married is going to have a miserable time," he'd said. He asked her if she would see a doctor he would recommend to her, and she'd said, "To get rid of the swelling?" He looked at me then and said, "As I was saying, that young man's going to have a miserable time."

'I asked him if there was anything I could do about her, and he said he hoped her condition would remain latent. Anyhow, he gave me plenty to think about.'

'We were used to her behaviour,' Jane said. 'I often felt sorry for Father, and yet he was the only one who could calm her. "Now, now, Meg," he used to say in his quiet voice.' A thought struck her. 'Aunt Mary, do you think she might be getting worse because of her age, you know, the menopause?'

'I suppose that's possible. Anyhow, if you take my advice, don't go back and live with her. Stick to your man.'

'I'll have a talk with John and see if he can think of someone who could help her. He's very clever, and now that he's a doctor . . .' A thought struck her. 'Do you think that was why she turned against him?'

'Who knows? It could be, or else the thought of being alone when you were gone. He was the one who was taking you away . . . Dr Nesbitt's dead now, or I could have asked him if her illness – if you could call it that – was progressive . . .'

'I'm glad you've told me this, Aunt –' Jane leaned forward and patted her knee – 'it helps me to understand her, and pity her.'

'If I were you I'd try to clear out.'

'Clear out?'

'I mean, don't live too near.'

That night, in the big, cold bed, and snuggled against each other, she told John what her aunt had told her about her mother.

'It explains a lot,' he said. 'I've got something to tell you. Remember that job I applied for before we came here? I got a letter today offering me the post.'

'The one in the mental hospital?

'Yes, it's not ideal, but we've no money so I think I'll have to take it until I get something better.'

'It's ridiculous that I had to leave my job, isn't it?'

'As if it was a sin to get married!'

'Maybe the rules will change with the war being on. Do you think they'll keep you in this job?'

'No, it's temporary. I'm ripe for cannon fodder.'

'Don't talk like that. Well, you'd better take it. I'll tell Aunt Mary we'll be leaving tomorrow.'

'She's been good to us, and I've enjoyed the young company. Great fun. And the big bed. Even though it was cold. Those sheets!'

'We had each other to keep us warm.'

'Darling –' he took her in his arms – 'life's been difficult for you since you met me. Your mother, and now a temporary job which won't keep me out of the war . . .'

14

'Life's been wonderful. I've met you. I need someone to support me.'

They were given a good send-off by all the family the following morning, Aunt Mary and Uncle Joe telling them that they would always find a home with them, and with good wishes ringing in their ears, they boarded the train for Glasgow, where they got a bus to Lanarkshire and the mental hospital.

After Glasgow, the market town where it was situated seemed dull. The first blow when they got to the hospital was to be told by the secretary that wives weren't allowed to live on the premises. In fact, he said, as if he was enjoying teasing them, that celibacy was ordained for the junior members of the staff. Only the superintendent was granted married quarters. No use to complain. It was the regulations and, as John was liable for call-up at any time, he was lucky to have a job at all.

The result was that Jane had to make her way back to the town and find a room in a commercial hotel. The stoicism which had been inculcated in her stood her in good stead as she unpacked her bag. The only consolation was that it could have been much worse. John might be in the Army. They would have to get out of this situation, or her mother would suggest that she should go back to her. She needn't know, she told herself.

John soon found out that they were not alone in their quandary. There were other members of the medical staff in the same position, who had decided that there was no point in protesting to the county council. Most of them were liable for call-up at any time and considered they were lucky to have a job.

He took this situation badly. Jane, because of her

15

upbringing, was prepared to be stoical. John was not. He was now a married man and, full of righteous indignation, he soon found a compromise between the restrictions of the powers-that-be and his natural desire to wallow in connubial bliss.

Jim, the butler, who supervised the doctors' common room, would smuggle Jane into the hospital in the evening, and see that she was safely escorted to the bus the following morning. It was foolproof, he pointed out, intimating that a backhander would oil the process. Twice-weekly visits were arranged, and William, the office clerk, kept the keys of the main gate, so he also had to be involved.

Picture Jane, then, following William down the middle of the hospital drive in the early morning. 'Follow the white line . . . All the way . . .' William sang, doing just that, and turning occasionally to beckon Jane at his heels. 'Hurry up, darling, you'll miss the bus!' William was a stabilised patient, and a homosexual. He called everyone 'darling' even the superintendent, a stern elderly man of Puritanical principles.

As William helped Jane on to the bus, he shouted, so that everyone inside could hear, 'Any time you want a bit of hanky panky, darling, just let me know.' His safe escort through the thickly-wooded grounds had possibly saved her from the clutches of a psychopath on the prowl, but it didn't save her blushes as she made her way to an empty seat.

The arrangement for Jane had its drawbacks despite her stoicism. Apart from her hospital visits, for the rest of the time she had to fill in her days in the dreary market town and in the drearier small hotel where she had a room, and where she was reduced to holding the corners of sheets with the two maids who seemed to be eternally washing and ironing them after the visits of commercial travellers who were their chief customers.

She railed against having had to give up her excellent and well-paid job because of protocol, and that she had no other choice than to spend hours in a draughty town hall rolling bandages for non-existent casualties. The ordeal of the Blitz on British towns was temporarily over.

Concentration was now on the Middle East, the start of the war in Burma, and in building up a triumphant force which would return to France and avenge Dunkirk.

Naturally, it wasn't long before her conscience began to trouble her about her mother. She had time on her hands; she ought to go and see her. To her surprise, when she did, she was received by a smiling, pleasant woman, who welcomed her as if there had never been any scenes, enquired about John, and invited Jane to bring him the next time she came. When she told John about this, he said, having acquired some knowledge from dealing with disturbed patients, 'I don't trust her. Her scheme is to make you think nothing has happened, so that you doubt your own senses. The minds of people like your mother are twisted.'

'Don't compare her with your patients,' she said. 'You'll be giving me a name for her condition soon.'

'I can give you one already,' he said. 'Paranoid psychophrenia.'

'Oh, John!' she said, laughing at him.

John was fairly happy with the temporary arrangement he had made. He loved Jane desperately, but he had the view of most young men of his age in wartime. If he hadn't been called up yet, it would come. He was sanguine about this. He had been allowed to finish his studies, but at the back of his mind was the feeling that the war wouldn't really get going until he was in it to lend a hand. Live for the present, he thought, he was only twenty-five, he was in love, and meantime he was married to the most wonderful girl in the world, and they would make the best of it.

Two

1971
Such enthusiasm, Jane thought, nearly thirty years later, for living and loving, for taking chances, all one's feelings intensified: black despair and flaming, upsurging joy – like those poppies in the garden below burning into one's senses.

The shade of the *bolet*, a stone veranda indigenous to the houses in south-west France, was welcome on such a hot June day. Now she could feel a gentle wind on her cheeks. And the view was better from here than from the rough grass which aproned the cottage. She never tired of it, truly pastoral, fields gently dipping and rising, dotted by sheep, defined by the bottle-green of hedges, with the round chateau tower of Gramon shimmering on the horizon. John and she had agreed that it was the house they had been looking for when they discovered it. They had come to the conclusion that they had to get away from the practice at least once a year, and it had been the retreat they had dreamt of, affordable, and French – they had both shared a passion for France for many years, and it was the only foreign language they had any command of.

It's close to peace, she told herself, and a place where I have many pleasant memories of John. She had decided a

19

year after his death to come here. It was familiar, a
second home, having been coming to Laborie for many
years. Scott, their son, aged twenty-eight, was now
married, and living in London with Valerie, his new
wife, both quietly dedicated, working in the same hospital, each at their own speciality. 'Nothing would make
me become a G.P. after seeing Dad ground down by it,'
he had said.

No need to worry about Scott and Valerie, planners, no
children until they were fully established and could afford a
house in Notting Hill, or some other salubrious area.

How different it had been at the start of our marriage,
she thought.

The joy when John had been offered a job as assistant
with view to a practice in Northern England, the guilty
feeling she had had when she had told her mother she was
moving away, then the tragic news coming to them a few
days later that her mother had been found dead in her
flat, having swallowed the contents of a bottle of sleeping
pills. John's family had supported her, and insisted that
they go on with their plans, Aunt Mary and Uncle Joe
had come from Fifeshire and taken care of all the
arrangements for the funeral and disposing of her
mother's flat and furniture, so that she and John could
be in Tynebay on time. She had been pregnant with
Scott, and the shock of her mother's death had made her
ill, and probably coloured her opinion of their new home.
How patient John was with me, she thought, putting up
with my self-reproachments, making arrangements for
our departure for England, promising her they would
have a holiday in France as soon as they could. He would
show it to her. He knew France well, having worked
there during vacations.

20

She fingered the folder on her lap containing the scribbled notes she had collected, written to assuage her grief, her regret, and her guilt when John had died. Her chief reason for coming here had been to collate them and type them out, make some sort of book of them to expunge that grief.

Perhaps, she had thought at the time, if I write it down, live through it, I'll find out where I went wrong, and quell my secret fear that I might become like my mother.

And this poem she had written this morning, like a warming-up exercise, or an attempt to drag her mind back to the present, as it was still with the past even today as she remembered their youthful passion in that narrow bed for celibate doctors, the glow still with her the following morning as she hobbled through the early mist behind William. Young love could be rough love.

How greedy they had been, how eager. Surely Scott wasn't as calm as he looked, there must be some of his father's passion behind that professional demeanour.

Her eyes fell again on the flaming clump of poppies at the foot of the steps, a brilliant burning scarlet. Through the dancing motes in front of her eyes as she looked up, she saw Boris coming across the rough grass lawn, and she waved her sheet of paper. 'Come up here, it's cool!'

They had known Boris and Hazel for a long time now, had first met them when both couples were staying at a small hotel in St. Martin, the village nearest Laborie, their own hamlet. The Halliwells had been looking for land on which to build, John and Jane for a cottage to buy. They had both got their wish eventually, the Maxwells their cottage in Laborie, the Halliwells a piece of land from the farmer, a few hundred yards from the Maxwells' cottage.

Now, at fifty-eight, Boris had retired, and he hoped at
last to finish building his house and give up living in the
caravan he had installed at the back of his property.
Hazel had long ago given up on it, and when she came
with Boris from London stayed in the St. Martin hotel,
driving around to see the various friends she had made
over the years. She still preferred London's Primrose
Hill.

John had called her the Urban Villager, and Scott had
referred to Boris' mess of bricks and timbers, which
seemed sometimes as far as he got, as the House that
Boris Never Built.

Boris came up the stone steps and collapsed on a
deckchair beside her. 'What have you got there? More
of your scribblings?'

'Such encouragement! It's a poem about these poppies.
It just welled up and spilled on to the page.'

'Let's see it.' She handed him the sheet of paper. He
put on his spectacles.

'Les Pivoines,' he intoned.

'Laborie peonies,
Loll in the sun's heat,
Exult in it, revel in it,
Turn on their stalks in it,
Neon-lit, fritillaried,
Black-dark in their cushioned hearts,
Wax purple-pink in it,
Pulsate and pant in it,
Wane to limp silk in it,
Let loose their petals,
Fall and then die.

'Yes, I get the message. Like butterflies. At least it's
got a beginning and an end, more than my house has.

Hazel will be here next week. She refuses to stay in the caravan any more. She's booked in again at the hotel.'

'So you won't be able to sleep together,' she said.

He glanced at her with a slight look of surprise. 'Doesn't matter now. She's not interested.'

'Where does all that ardour go? Time was . . .'

She thought of that narrow bed in the mental hospital. And that rather tactless remark of hers to Boris. What had got into her? 'Who cares if it's narrow,' John had said. 'We make a good sandwich.' Those few months had been episodic for both of them. When she looked back on them, she thought of love, only love.

She said aloud, 'I'm trying to write about it, the impermanency, the poignancy, like those poppies.'

'What's *it*?'

'Youth.'

'Might be better than this.' He gave back the sheet of paper to her. 'Bit twee?'

She took it, thinking you could never take offence at Boris. His grin was beguiling, warm, impish, a grin rather than a sedate smile. Now, although his years had given him added girth, the charm of that grin remained.

And it worked as well with men. Jane had seen him chatting to Benoit, the farmer, on the High Field where he grew his tobacco plants and where she often walked, had heard the farmer's appreciative laughter, '*Ah, bon!*' Neither spoke the other's language well, besides Benoit's was largely patois, Languedoc. Between them there was what she thought of as the language of the soul.

'Have you settled down now?' Boris asked.

'Oh, yes. There's always a great feeling of relief when decisions are made. I'm actually basking in that now.'

'Scott got the job he wanted in London?'

'Yes. Both of them. In the same hospital. And they're negotiating for a house they've seen in Notting Hill. They're single-minded and they seem to have the same views on everything. It should be a successful marriage.'

'Wasn't yours? I always thought of you as a really happy couple.'

'We were happy here. There were . . . difficult periods, though, where we lived. But then G.P.'s don't have much time for introspection. That's left to the wives, although they're almost as busy. There were certain times – the war, for instance, and my mother's suicide – that created problems.' Don't say too much to this man with the grin that wins you over. 'But, on the whole, yes, it was a happy marriage.'

'I wouldn't say that about ours. Hazel and I fight like cats and dogs. We differ in most things. This land and the time I spend on it is a constant irritation to her. It was better at the beginning. There were the making-up times, hectic . . . Now she's uninterested.'

'Perhaps if you'd had children?'

'She has some gynaecological irregularity. Wouldn't have it seen to. She never saw herself as a mother.'

'Ah, well . . .' Jane herself had seen it as inevitable. Perhaps all girls did in wartime. 'Perhaps you'll make such a cracking job of the house, now you've more time, that she'll be charmed.'

'She doesn't understand my wish to use my hands. I made enough money in the city to employ people instead. The house could have been up years ago if I'd hired builders, but I didn't want to. No, she's never really liked being here. Too rural, boring peasants – excluding you and John, of course. She liked that couple we met at the hotel.'

24

'Raoul and Margo. They split up.'

'Yes, I remember. She would have preferred St. Tropez.'

'I never felt like that. I was glad to buy this cottage, even when we could ill afford it. I used to dream of Laborie in that cold, miserable north-east town where we lived.'

Jane looked to her left, past the drying-green, down the short hill to the huddle of houses at its foot, a faux chateau-type house where Mr Graf had lived – it had been built for the old man by some builders in Cahors – the half-built walls of Boris' house, the two old cottages opposite of honey-coloured stone like their own, the Lamartines' and the Croziers', then past them to Benoit's farm, a pleasing honey-coloured huddle of buildings. The turn of the rough road and the bend where the farm seemed to burrow into the fields was satisfying to the eye, a painter could paint it. A picture you could walk into.

The road caught the golden glow from the fading sun, and the trees were darkly green, and there was Caesar, the farm dog stretched out in the heat in the middle of the road. Old dogs liked heat.

This was now her real home, their house in Tynebay just a staging-post, although she had lived there from 1943 until John's death when he was fifty-four. This was the present, that was the past; two lives.

But there was a deeper division. There was the outward life, the one people saw and on which they made their judgements, and the inner one, where the real you lived, that was what mattered. She had thought that maybe she would unearth that inner one, that deeper one, through being here.

It was strange that she hadn't wished to return to

Scotland where her roots were. But it hadn't been a happy life until she met John, and that had been of short duration. There was her mother's death, and she had found it hard to forgive Robert for not coming home to be at the funeral. He had sloughed off his ties with Scotland. Then she had lost a friend in Elma. Bob had been killed in Anzio and she had met an American, becoming like many Glasgow girls a G.I. bride, and going back with him to New York. She had stopped replying to Jane's letters, her life there must have been too engrossing.

Boris sloped off – he was the kind of man who 'sloped off' – and she went into the cool kitchen to fetch the milk jug. She usually walked down to the farm about this time, five o'clock, for a fresh supply, it was her time for making a public appearance. Then there would be the leisurely drink on the *bolet*, perhaps, or down the steep stone steps to the rough grass lawn, afterwards to potter round the beds of lupins, poppies, petunias, a welter of perennials broken up by the scatter of annuals which she had sown earlier.

Flowers grew easier here, but didn't last long. Like the poppies. Yes, the poem had been a bit twee. And gardens didn't demand the same attention here as they did in England, with the compulsive attention to neat edges, grass cutting and weeding. Here she just did a nightly watering.

On the way down the hill she was stopped by Madame Haguet and her flock of sheep which she brought down from the high *causse* each evening; those rocky highlands where the sweet-smelling thyme grew. She apologized for the small traffic jam with her usual courtesy. And with her usual greeting, '*Ça va bien, madame?*'

Jane, as usual, brought up the subject of the weather, because one always talked about the weather in England and she hadn't broken herself of the habit. She imagined Madame Haguet was slightly amused by this, but on the other hand she always sported a long black dusty umbrella which served a dual purpose when she was sitting in the sun on the hillside with her flock.

Neither Madame Lamartine nor Madame Crozier were in their gardens, perhaps because Jane was a little later than usual. Monsieur Crozier was an assistant in *la Maison de la Presse* in Gramon (and kindly brought her an English paper if requested), and Madame Lamartine, a sprightly old lady of over eighty, lived with her daughter and son-in-law, or the other way round as she always referred to '*ma maison*'. She'd had to accept the fact that her daughter, who'd had a man friend for an unconscionable time, would leave her to look after herself unless Marie's intended was invited to join the household. Fortunately Madame had found to her surprise that Jean was a decided adjunct to the family, doing all the heavier tasks which she was finding difficult.

Madame Lisieux, Benoit's wife, was milking when Jane arrived, her broad haunches bulging over the stool. 'Ah, Madame Maxwell,' she cried, the side of her face against the cow's flank. '*Comme d'habitude!*'

'*Oui, Madame, c'est moi.* Agnès isn't back yet?' This was her married daughter who lived in St. Martin, but who still helped her mother on the farm. 'Has the baby arrived?'

'Yes, a beautiful baby girl. Well, one isn't surprised, of course.' Jane guessed the latter remark referred to the fact that when Agnès and Guy had been courting, her parents had installed them in the farm's empty *gîte*. The

French were forever practical in their outlook. Perhaps they had wanted Guy to prove his manhood. She changed the subject.

'Monsieur Graf's house is still empty?'

'Yes, we miss the old gentleman pottering about. He used to bring cabbage stalks to feed my rabbits. He loved them. I never forgot him when I was making a pie.'

'Will the house be sold?'

'No, it's been left to his nephew. And here is the news! I've had a letter asking me to air it and get in some necessities for the kitchen. I always did it for Monsieur Graf when he was back in Holland.'

Jane nodded. She remembered he had been Dutch, a people who seemed to like this part of France. 'Will they use it as a holiday house, do you think?' Madame shook her head.

'*Qui le sait?* All I know is that the three of them are arriving tomorrow.'

'The three of them?'

'Yes, I should say, the four of them, the nephew and his wife and daughter, and the daughter's baby.'

'*Ah, bon!*' She hid her surprise.

When she walked back up the hill she glanced at the Graf house, spick and span with its terrace, its *pigeonnier*, and to the left of it Boris' half-built edifice. Would his new neighbours object to the untidiness? Old Monsieur Graf had taken a great interest in it.

Boris was nowhere to be seen. He would be in his caravan preparing his supper which he enjoyed doing. He had a talent for cooking, copying French cuisine. He sometimes invited her to sample it.

Even in a backwater like this, she thought, there were changes. Now two babies, that of Agnès, the Lisieux's

28

daughter, and the baby granddaughter of the new Monsieur Graf.

Scott's had been a difficult birth, she thought, remembering that nightmare journey to the nursing home. John had said 'never again', as if he had given birth himself, all his medical knowledge gone by the board. She went on up the hill towards her own cottage, stepping aside to avoid the tractor which Jean-Claude, from one of the farms beyond Benoit's, was driving in his usual brigandish fashion. He had two children sitting beside him, and they all waved, Jean-Claude with an extravagant sweep of the hand, as if they were meeting in Bond Street. '*Bon appetit!*'

The mosquitoes drove her in, reluctantly, as she sat later with her drink. She had enjoyed watching the lights flickering on one by one in distant Gramon, in the chateau perched on top with its wall spiraling up the hillside. 'Safe from the English,' John had joked.

She was fortunate that she enjoyed solitude. Scott, being sensitive, had recognized this, and had not demurred when she'd told him of her decision to come to Laborie to live. 'Give it a year,' he'd said, 'and in the meantime Valerie and I will keep our eyes open for a small flat. If we buy a large house you might install yourself there from time to time instead. See a bit of life.' But all life is here, she thought. It's inside me, hidden, and the words occurred to her: 'a hidden narrative' which only she could explore because it was hers.

Three

Her mother's suicide was a tragic beginning to their marriage, to any marriage, but she had promised her aunt that she would go on with her life, and not spoil John's. His mother had said as much, indeed there was no end to good advice, but John was her support, her anchor. His buoyancy of spirit cheered her, inspired her, decided her to do what everyone else did when struck by tragedy, to get on with life. Other people had suffered as she suffered, it was up to her not to let them down. I have joined the coterie of smiling faces, she thought, smiling to hide their grief, and I have something which perhaps they didn't have, John . . .

Gaunt, Jane thought, looking at the square red-brick house with the flat windows bordered in pale sandstone. Gaunt, and mean, and ugly.

'In we go,' John said, putting down the suitcase he was carrying to ring the doorbell.

'Do you like it?' she said, thinking, it's not important. Don't go by first impressions. And no doubt *they* could have looked smarter. Being short of money – a chronic state with them – they had rigged up a small tent they carried in the boot of the car and spent last night in some

30

unidentifiable part of the countryside outside Newcastle. A cow had blundered against the side of the tent waking them from sleep and scaring the life out of her. The baby, she had thought, I don't want the baby hurt.

The door was opened by a plump, pasty-faced young woman with frizzy carrot-coloured hair. 'Is it Dr and Mrs Maxwell?' She peered through glasses. 'Come in, please.'

They followed her into a terrazzo-floored hall, gloomy because of the closed mahogany doors. On one of them was inscribed 'Waiting Room', the others had doctors' names on them.

'Dr Moir is consulting at the moment,' she said. 'I'll tell him you're here. He may want to see you before you go upstairs. Please take a seat.' She indicated a bench, throwing a meaningful glance, Jane thought, at her bulging stomach.

'We must look sights,' she said, smiling at John, remembering to smile. His shirt looked creased, as did his jacket, his curly hair hadn't had its usual subjection to water and a stiff brush. She probably wasn't very glamorous herself with her crumpled skirt, and jacket which barely met at the front.

The young woman reappeared. 'Dr Moir will be here shortly. Please excuse me. I must get on.' She disappeared into a room at the end of the hall and shut the door behind her.

'Dispensary,' John said, reading the inscription on it. 'I bet they make up the medicine themselves.'

'I thought she might have offered us a cup of tea. I'm starving.'

'We'll do that for ourselves when we get up to our own quarters. Think of it, Jane, our own place, a double bed!' She loved him with her glance.

'You're a randy old thing. Think where that has led us.' She laid her hand on her stomach. At that moment one of the doors burst open and a smallish, thin-faced man came hurrying towards them.

'I'm Dr Moir.' He held out his hand. 'Dr and Mrs Maxwell? I'm a bit rushed. Huge surgery as usual.' His thin face stretched in a mirthless smile. 'Supposing you go upstairs and look around for an hour, then I'd like you to come down again, Dr Maxwell, and I'll give you your list of visits. Make it less than an hour if you can. Time's a precious commodity here. I've been running this place single-handed for the last week.' He strode towards the door at the foot of the hall, opened it and called in. 'Miss Wilmot! Show them upstairs, will you? I have to get back.' He went swiftly past John and Jane, giving them a brief, decisive nod and disappeared through the door he had come from.

'This way, please.' The young woman was at their side. 'By the way, I'm Miss Wilmot, but you can call me Esther. Everyone else does.' But not Dr Moir, Jane thought.

'Right-oh!' John said. He picked up the suitcase, and together they followed Esther Wilmot's swaying rump up a steep flight of stairs. John put a sympathetic hand under Jane's elbow. Halfway up there was a landing with a glass door and she could see through it a small wrought-iron platform with the top of a staircase showing, which might, hopefully, lead to a back garden.

Upstairs was certainly spacious, if shabby. The walls were all coloured beige with a dado of diamond-patterned brown shiny wallpaper, and there was a preponderance of prints on the walls of many-funnelled, many-

32

tiered ocean-going liners hung at regular intervals. 'Where there's muck, there's money,' John commented.

The furniture was heavy but ponderously comfortable, cushioned in brown velvet, and 'the doctor's bedroom', as Esther Wilmot had called it, was large with a huge double bed. On the wall above the side-table, there was hanging an open-ended flexible tube. 'What on earth is that?' Jane asked. 'Is it some weird medical instrument?'

He laughed. 'I've heard of them. Antediluvian. No, it's a speaking tube.' They had both flopped down on the bed immediately Esther Wilmot had left them. 'There will be a hole on the outside wall beside the main door and the patient speaks, or shouts into it, usually in the middle of the night, when he needs a doctor.' He put his arm round her. 'Just when we might be otherwise engaged . . .'

'What a hope!'

'I thought they'd gone out with the Ark.'

'Not in Tynebay, evidently. We must get up.' She kissed him and heaved herself off the bed. 'I feel more cheerful now. I hate that state of homelessness, the in-between stage. Must be the nesting instinct. Now that we've got a place of our own, it's fine.'

'You weren't impressed at the beginning.'

'Not especially. It was foolish to expect a country cottage here with roses round the door.' But she still thought the whole atmosphere was depressing, and her hopes that Dr Moir would turn out to be affable and outgoing had been dashed right away by his stretched, mirthless smile and his fussiness. He could have shown more interest in them. And a blind man could see she was pregnant.

They had tea in the large kitchen. Someone had

stocked it with the necessities of existence – possibly the indispensable Esther Wilmot – and they had toast and marmalade with lots of hot tea. John was ready to go downstairs again in little over half an hour, and she had also persuaded him to subdue his unruly hair with water from the kitchen tap. He looked very handsome, and carefree – when he must be apprehensive – his chin up and his eyes smiling, and she hoped that Dr Moir, of the stretched mirthless smile, wouldn't douse his joie de vivre too quickly. 'Go to it,' she laughed, kissing him.

But they had a job, and they were together. And the baby would soon be here, and perhaps they'd be lucky and he would be considered to be doing essential work, and avoid calling-up. But she knew he wanted to go. And she dreaded losing his support.

She cleared away the remains of their simple meal, washing up at the sink which was underneath the window. The view was not inspiring, a concreted courtyard with a garage opening on to it, no sign of a garden, the whole surrounded by a high brick wall with broken glass embedded on its top. Barlinnie, she thought, remembering the notorious Glasgow prison. Would this place become the same, especially if she were left here on her own? Well, I shan't have to listen to Mother's criticisms. The thought flashed through her mind, making her feel ashamed.

The fire was laid in the large sitting room which looked on to the street, but she decided to wait until later to light it. Coal would be in short supply even here. She unpacked the suitcase, set up their wedding photograph and hung up their clothes. It was an adventure. She had always wanted to live in England, although her England was one of gracious London terraces, parks where people rode their horses, or, if the country, white-washed cottages round a village green. The inevitable duck pond. She had thought of a gentle landscape, gentle sunshine, voices which were more melodious than those she had grown up with. She realized that her impressions had been gained from novels written by middle-class women about English middle-class people, but the impression was still there.

This was reality, a mining, ship-building industrial part of England, not unlike Glasgow in many ways; it had been foolish to expect it to be any different. Beggars can't be choosers, she told herself, as she prepared herself to venture forth and find the shops. She was the homemaker.

'You'll never guess what I saw in the butcher's today,' she said to John over a very late supper. There had been no interval between afternoon and evening surgery – she had guessed that by the ceaseless ringing of the door bell – and lunch had consisted of a sandwich which he had eaten standing at the kitchen table.

'What?' He looked tired out and his face was slightly grubby. Coal-mining country, she thought. There had been no time all day for even a cursory wash.

'A sheep's head! Dripping with blood!'

'Grisly. I know they're queer folks but they don't eat sheep's heads for God's sake.'

'No, I asked the butcher. They cost only one shilling and people boil them for hours and hours and then scrape the brains out and serve them with caper sauce. Might be quite nice.'

'No, thanks, I'll stick to this.' But she noticed the chop she had cooked for him was half-eaten and the vegetables pushed to one side.

'Aren't you hungry?'

'Past it, I think, but the patients are very kind. I had several offers of tea which I didn't accept.'

'What do you think of Dr Moir?'

'I scarcely saw him. He certainly wasn't there at the afternoon surgery.'

'Maybe he went home for a rest?'

'Oh, I don't think so. Esther told me he lives on the other side of Newcastle, some posh suburb, I expect. She's becoming quite chatty.'

'Your fatal charm.'

'That's it. But, yes, the patients are very nice. One of them gave me a cabbage from his allotment. "For Mrs Doctor Maxwell," he said. That's your title, presumably, around these parts.'

'Rather nice. I had a walk around when I was out. There isn't much to see, rows and rows of terrace houses running down to the river. The road this house is on meets with the coastal road further up. It would be nice to go there sometime, see the sea.'

'The shore will all be guarded by barbed wire. They're expecting trouble here sooner or later, so Dr Moir told me. He gave me a tin hat to keep in the car.'

'You must let me see it when you bring up the cabbage. Do you really like him, John?'

'He's quite polite –' he met Jane's eyes – 'but, well, he's not exactly a bundle of fun. Still, he's been rushed off his feet, and temps are never allowed to stay long. He's put in an appeal for me, he says.'

'Oh, that's good! That's sufficient, isn't it?'

'No, it isn't sufficient, darling. I feel the same about leaving you, but I know I'll have to go sooner or later.'

'And see some of the action?' It was a phrase she had heard him use.

'I want to be here with you when the baby comes.'

'Well, that's good enough.' She got up. 'I tell you what, I'll clear up and you go and have a bath then we'll get into bed. Everything will be all right there.'

'Yes, it's always all right there.' He put his arms round her, carefully. 'You must be fed up.'

'Just a little. You can squeeze a bit, dirty-face.'

The comfort, the expanse, and the coziness of being together in such a generous bed lulled them to sleep almost immediately. It seemed seconds later that they were both wakened by a shrill voice which echoed round the room, filling it. Jane's heart leapt into her throat with fear.

'Will the doctor come to Mrs Batty, 3, Newton Terrace, right away?' The voice was trembling. 'Me mam has had a . . .' There were muttered voices in the background, then the first one came back again, half-crying this time: 'Me mam has had a . . . a . . . haemorrhage!'

'Probably a bloody nosebleed,' John muttered. He rolled out of bed and fumbled for his trousers. 'Now you know what the medical instrument –' he glanced at the speaking-tube aperture – 'is for . . .'

Four

1943

John hesitated at the entrance to the village green – Jane always said it was the only decent part of the town – then drove in and stopped at one of the double-fronted brick villas. He got out of the car, went quickly up the gravel path, which bisected a neat garden, and rang the doorbell. He really ought to have gone straight home, but he might as well look in on the Cains – they were a decent couple. Mrs Cain opened the door and greeted him, looking pleased.

'Come in, doctor! Norman will be glad to see you. He hasn't been so well today.'

'Sorry to hear that,' he said, following her into the sitting room. Everything shone, the ornaments, the furniture, the pictures were lit from above, the standard lamp glowed rosily, competing with the fire. Their own room seemed gloomy as he compared it in his mind. The dull brown leather upholstery, and the velvet cushions of the same colour absorbed what light there was from a central bulb, covered by a pale beige shade. There had never been enough money to make any changes, and Moir was a skinflint.

Jane bought some flowers occasionally to brighten it up – he himself was kept so busy that he never got near the shops. Besides, a coming baby seemed to require a bigger wardrobe than either of them possessed for themselves.

Norman Cain got up to greet him, his face prematurely lined for his fifty-five years, and his hand felt chalky in John's grasp. 'Am I glad you looked in, doctor!'

'Just what you were hoping for, dear,' Mrs Cain said, beaming. 'I'll go and make a cup of tea while you have your little consultation . . .'

'Please, no,' John said, holding up his hand. 'I must get back to Jane . . .'

'Of course you must, but it won't take a minute.' She went quickly out of the room and he gave up trying to stop her. He thought of the trolley she would wheel in laden with its fine bone china, its silver tea service, and that home-made lemon sponge of hers with the cream filling and the lemon-flavoured icing. He'd give his back teeth for a slice of it right now.

'Any more palpitations, Mr Cain? he asked, taking the seat the man indicated.

'No, I must say I've been free of those thanks to that specialist you recommended, but principally to you. If you've got faith in your doctor . . .' He looked at John who felt himself basking in the man's appreciation. A little praise never did anyone any harm. 'But to tell you the truth' – now for the moan – 'I've been a little, well, down, today. You said to stay off for a month and the specialist agreed, but I worry about the department. Without boasting, they can't do without me.' He was head clerk in one of the shipbuilding yards.

'Have you tried having a walk every day? Fresh air's the best remedy for you now. A little gentle exercise and some fresh air into your lungs.' The room was over-heated for a start.

'I don't seem to have the energy, doctor.'

'A little spin out in the car? Do you get petrol for it?'

'Some, but you've got to be careful in a town like this, people talk, think you're being favoured . . .' Which you probably are, John thought. Dr Moir kept a careful note of the petrol *he* used, and he knew Jane only lit the fire in the evenings for him coming home, which made him feel guilty.

The door opened and Mrs Cain came in pushing the laden trolley. He spotted his favourite sponge cake, and as well there were those chocolate things made with cornflakes in paper cups, and brandy snaps stuffed with coffee-coloured cream. He mentally licked his lips.

'You know the way to a man's heart,' he said, as he stood up to help her.

'I know your favourite. A slice of lemon sponge to begin with, and I'll put your cup on this little table at your elbow, doctor. That's right. The same for you, Norman?'

'I think I could manage a brandy snap, dear.'

'Delicious,' John said, using one of the silver cake knives to cut a portion off his generous slice of cake.

'I expect your poor little wife isn't feeling like baking at the moment. I've made two lemon sponges this after-noon, and one is for her. A little bird must have told me you'd be looking in.'

'That's very kind. Yes, you're right. Jane's feeling the last weeks particularly trying.'

'Ah.' Her eyes shone. 'But think of the joy ahead, a joy unfortunately, which Norman and I never knew.' Mr Cain kept his head down.

'We can't all be blessed,' he mumbled into the hon-eycombed toffee roll. John experienced a sudden longing for those early days in the single bed at the hospital when he and Jane had been first married. What carefree joy that had been. What abandon. Not like now in this dreary little town with the crippling workload foisted on him.

'But he's a changed man recently,' his wife said. 'Just look at him!' John looked and was not unduly impressed by the hunched thin figure with the sparse hair and the lined face. 'You have the magic touch, Dr Maxwell.'

Mr Cain straightened up, wiping his fingers delicately on the linen embroidered napkin. There was a piece of toffee trembling on his lip. 'That's it, the magic touch. Some have it, some haven't.' He looked regretful. John remembered he and Jane had once joked about the hundreds of putative babies which hadn't been given the 'Go' sign, as she had put it. The magic touch indeed. 'You always buck me up, doctor. I was feeling a little low . . .'

His wife interrupted him. 'He sits moping at the fire, doctor. I tell him and tell him . . .' Her voice was querulous.

'You don't understand the worries a man in my position has . . . Dr Maxwell does. A man of talent. Not only has he cured me – freshen the doctor's cup, Mary – but he opens new vistas. Remember the last time you were here, doctor, you were telling us about the mental hospital you worked in. Your experience there must have been an eye-opener for you.'

John regretted that confidence. 'Yes, indeed.' Good tea, too. Not stewed. 'I read quite a lot on the speciality when I was there. Expected to. Well, thank you, Mrs Cain, I really shouldn't.' He accepted another generous slice of lemon sponge. 'I've a weakness for home-made cakes.' Jane always said she was a savoury person and didn't go in for too many sweet things.

'Nothing shop-bought in that department enters this house, doctor. Of course, sugar is difficult, but there are ways and means, if you've lived here a long time as we have.'

'Now, now, Mary, don't let our little secrets out of the bag.' Mr Cain held up a finger, and whether it was the glow of the fire or his lemon sponge, but John, looking at him, saw completely through him, deep down to his dissatisfaction with life, but principally with himself.

And what about you, he asked himself. Wasting your time here where you aren't really needed, when you should be with Jane. You know how she worries about her mother's suicide, although she doesn't say so. Pure cupboard love on your part, looking for a bit of pandering because you're not getting it at home. There was nothing more he could do for this man.

'Can you remember the titles of some of the books you had to read, doctor? I'm a great reader myself.' I'll tell him in a minute. Be brutally frank. He heard his own voice.

'Oh,' he said airily, 'Nicole's *Psycho-pathology of the Mind*, Jung, Freud, Adler, all that sort of stuff . . .' He saw the rapt attention he was being given by his two listeners, and tried to visualize the contents of the bookcase in the doctors' common room at the hospital which they'd hardly ever opened.

'How you absorb all that knowledge!' Mr Cain turned to his wife. 'Wonderful, isn't it, Mary?' She nodded, eyes wide.

'Is there any book you could recommend to me,

doctor?' he went on. 'I've always been interested in the workings of the human mind . . .'

Too damn interested, John thought. Neurotic's more like it.

'There's White's *Outline of Psychiatry*, but for the layman, no, Mr Cain, best to leave it to the professionals . . .' Give up this nonsense. Tell him to get back to work and stop thinking about himself. 'You had to know, of course, which drugs to use. Most of the patients were stabilised.' He thought of William. 'Others could be dangerous. I remember one of them lunging at me with a knife he'd stolen from the kitchen. You had to have eyes in the back of your head.'

'That was really frightening!' Mrs Cain's rapt attention reminded him of his own mother and father, always ready to listen to him. They had never got over the fact that he was a qualified doctor, and yet they had made no demands on him when he married and moved away. They were the soul of propriety, always putting Jane first, never intruding, never offering unasked-for advice.

He ought to get back. Jane had been sorry for herself this morning, trying to curl up against him in bed, foiled by her swollen stomach, looking for comfort. 'Do you think I should be induced, John? It's past the date.'

And he'd said, only repeating what he'd heard Dr Moir say to patients, 'No, let nature take its course . . .'

He'd felt heartily sorry for her and here he was wasting time with this couple because of his own creature comforts. He got to his feet.

'I must go. Thank you so much, Mrs Cain. Now, Mr Cain, since you seem much better, I think you should get back to work next week. It's the best thing . . .'

'But, doctor' – he looked taken aback – 'you said . . .'

He spoke firmly. 'I've taken your blood pressure this evening and it's quite normal. I really think you'd be better off now resuming your normal duties . . .' You can't have your cake and eat it, Mr Cain, he said to himself, but wasn't he calling the pot black with the taste of the lemon sponge lingering on his taste buds?

'Well, the doctor is always right,' Mrs Cain said smoothly. 'What a pity you have to go, doctor, just when we were enjoying our little talk. Now you mustn't forget Mrs Maxwell's lemon . . .' The telephone bell shrilled in the hall. She got up and went out. There was an uncomfortable silence.

'So you think I ought to go back?' Mr Cain looked peeved, his mouth turned downwards.

'Yes, I really think so.' He was straining his ears to try and hear what Mrs Cain was saying. She burst into the room looking excited.

'It's your wife, Dr Maxwell!'

He was immediately alarmed, and guilty. 'Does she want me to speak?'

'Yes, I couldn't make her out, asking if you were here, I think . . .'

He was on his feet. 'Excuse me . . .' He half-ran into the hall and lifted the receiver. He could hardly recognize Jane's strangled voice at first.

'John, it's started! I was just preparing the supper and it started. I had to hang on to the kitchen table . . .'

His heart was thudding against his ribs. 'Are the pains coming regularly?'

'Yes, I think so.'

'Go and lie down and time them. I'll be back right away.'

The faces of Mr and Mrs Cain were full of concern

when he went back to the room. 'I have to get home right away. My wife's gone into labour.'

'My goodness, of course!' Mrs Cain said. 'I'll show you out.' If anything, Mr Cain looked disappointed. In the hall she said something about a lemon sponge, but he cut in. 'Don't bother, please. I must get home.' He opened the door and let himself out, ran down the drive, threw himself into the car, started it, and circled the green far too quickly, emerging into the main road which led to their house. He wondered if he should put on his tin hat as an excuse if he were seen breaking the speed limit.

When he reached the main door of the house he opened it and went bounding up the stairs two at a time. 'Jane!' he called. 'Where are you?'

'In here.' Her voice came from the kitchen. He burst into the room and found her sitting at the table. 'I couldn't get to the bedroom. I was just . . . oh!' She got up and tried to walk. He caught her in his arms.

'Don't panic.' He rubbed her back. She said, against him, 'I thought you'd be at the Cains. They take up too much of your time. What do you talk about for God's sake?'

'Nothing much. The man's been ill, but he's better now. I think we should get you to the nursing home right away. It's a good drive . . .'

'Not yet.' She drew away from him. 'Not yet, please. I feel not so bad now.' Her face was pathetic.

He smiled down at her, and kissed her. 'Tell you what. Come and lie down and I'll phone them, then I'll make you a cup of tea.'

'OK.'

He supported her back to their bedroom along the

45

semi-dark corridor. So poorly lit, he thought, transferring his guilt to Dr Moir and his meanness.

Because of the always imminent threat of bombing, the local nursing home had moved to an empty country mansion twelve miles out of Newcastle. Fortunately he got the matron right away.

'It's Dr Maxwell, matron. My wife's gone into labour.'

'She's late.' She sounded reproving, and he remembered their interview with her, a stout, stern-faced elderly woman who had looked at Jane in a disparaging fashion as if she thought the whole business of child-bearing was regrettable, especially in wartime.

'Bring her in then, doctor. I'll have a bed ready.' She hung up abruptly.

'Have I to go?' Jane asked, rising on her elbow.

'Yes, right away. But I'll have to ring Dr Moir and get calls transferred.'

'Well, do it quickly. Here's another one . . .' She rolled back on the bed, her knees pulled up. 'Couldn't you give me something?' She looked drawn and pale.

'No, it's risky.' He felt totally inadequate. Since he'd started in the practice he had been lucky enough to arrive at the address of the woman in labour when Mrs Robinson, the midwife, had done all that was necessary.

Dr Moir had never discussed Jane's pregnancy with him, but there was one golden rule. The premises must not be left unattended. If only he hadn't called in on the Cains, he might have caught Esther before she left and asked her to stand in for him.

He was dialling Dr Moir's number as he pondered. It was his wife who answered. He and Jane hadn't met her, but she had telephoned once or twice and said she was looking forward to them coming to their house when the baby had arrived. She had sounded more pleasant than her husband. 'It's John Maxwell, Mrs Moir,' he said.

'Oh, hello! Are you looking for my husband? I'm afraid he's gone to the garage to fill up his car. Is there anything I can do?'

'It's Jane. She's gone into labour. I must get her to the nursing home right away. Will you tell him?'

'Of course.' Pleasant, he thought, but withdrawn.

'There's no one else here . . .'

'Your wife comes first. The patients will just have to wait. I'll phone and have the calls transferred, I'll stand in for Esther. I hope there are no accidents.'

'Thanks.' He hung up. What a peculiar thing to say.

'It's all arranged, Jane.' He bent over her and kissed her. 'Where's your case, darling?' She looked young and frightened. He felt a masculine stab of guilt.

'In the corner over there.' She waved an arm weakly. How pale she looked. He felt totally inadequate, and as miserable as she looked. 'Was it Dr Moir?'

'No. Missus. She sent her best wishes. Try and get up. I'll help you. Put your arms round my neck. There, that's right.' He heaved her out of bed and helped her to stand upright. They laughed at each other and the tears sprang into her eyes. He could have had her halfway to the nursing home if he hadn't wasted time at the Cains. He cursed himself and his schoolboy greed and the stupid pleasure he took in their well-appointed home.

'I wish I had my mother with me,' she said, half-laughing, half-crying. 'Isn't that funny?'

'No, I don't think so. Natural. Anyhow, you've got me. I'll take care of you.'

'Like coming in late.'

47

'Don't rub it in. I'm sorry, very sorry.' The lemon taste still on his tongue from the sponge cake was like gall.

The city was busy with traffic and only lit enough to enable it to function, and he was glad when they had left it behind them and were speeding northwards through what seemed to be a long dark tunnel of trees.

'Gosh!' Jane said suddenly. 'I'm soaking! Is it blood?'

'No, it can't be.' He felt panic-stricken. What if there was some terrible emergency that he wasn't going to be able to deal with, and then he remembered. 'It's the membranes. They've ruptured.' That's bad, he thought. She's going to have a dry labour, and a first baby.

He thought for the first time of this small creature inside her struggling to get out, their baby, now made even more difficult . . . He remembered the only birth at the mental hospital, the result of one of the women patients being accosted in the woods by a male patient, and the terrible shrieks of her when she was in labour. It had taken himself and another doctor, Chalmers, he remembered he was called, to hold her down while another one – he couldn't remember his name – did the necessary. Banshee shrieks. The superintendent had been furious – not at the woman's agony – but that the escape of the couple from their respective wards had gone undetected.

'Will it make it more difficult?' Jane asked.

'I don't think so. But don't worry. The matron's an old hand at the game. Plenty of experience.'

'I didn't like her very much. She was fierce. I expect she's a frustrated old maid.'

'As long as she's capable. Is it bad, darling?' She had given a groan.

'Bad enough. But there's no way out of it. It's the . . .

inevitability. Are we nearly there?' And then: 'Do you think Dr Moir will be annoyed?'

'What about? He knows you're pregnant, for goodness sake! He ought to have discussed it with me, but he's so darned busy all the time, or thinks he is, rushing past you. I should have liked to ask him things but he always says, "Some other time, doctor." It's infuriating.'

'He's got a family, hasn't he? He must know what it's about.'

'I don't think so. And he's uncommunicative. But he doesn't do many confinements. Passes them all on to me. I'm the dogsbody.' He didn't say anything about Nurse Robinson who helped him and gave him the credit. A brick.

'We ought to have just had it at home. You could have done me.' Jane's voice was plaintive.

Done for you, he thought. 'It's not ethical,' he said. My precious lovely Jane. I wouldn't have risked it. What if he'd made a hash of it and something terrible had happened to her and this baby of theirs . . . 'There's a notice-board,' he said. 'I think it said Northcliffe Nursing Home. We're nearly there. Bear up.'

'It's bear down, really.' He squeezed her hand. His Jane. 'Oh, I'm very tired with all this,' she said, her voice was trembling. 'Mother didn't get time to discuss having babies with me, perhaps she would have liked that if . . . and there's no one in Tynebay.' Her voice was choked with sobs. 'And all the young people seem to be in the Forces, or munitions, and it's old people, like the Cains everywhere – whom you seem to like so much – or the men in the yards and their wives and children.'

'Here we are,' he said. 'You'll be all right, Jane. You're a brave girl.' He thankfully drove up a long dark drive.

The door opened when he rang and a young nurse greeted him. 'Is it Dr and Mrs Maxwell? Come in. Do you need a chair, Mrs Maxwell?'

'No, thanks.' Jane tried to straighten.

'Come away, then.' She took them along a corridor and into a bare room with a high bed and a couple of chairs. 'Please sit down, and I'll tell the matron you're here. Or better still, maybe you'd help her to undress, doctor – there's a gown there – and get her on to the bed. We're short-staffed.'

'Right-oh!' He began to assist Jane. 'Do-it-yourself here!'

'I hope all the good nurses aren't in the Forces.'

'I hope not.' He folded her sodden underclothes – not blood – and put them on the chair, then helped her into the gown and on to the bed.

'It's high,' she said. 'Supposing I roll off?'

'Maybe it's an examination couch and then you'll have a room. I booked one. Don't worry, darling. We'll have a lovely baby quite soon. What were the names you chose?'

'*You* know. Scott or Lesley. Remember we fixed it up in bed . . . after that night.'

'Yes, after . . . it should be a good baby, by God. I like both names, and I don't care which it is. Do you?'

'Men always want girls. I should like a son.' The door opened and the Amazonian figure of the matron seemed to fill the small room.

'Well, Dr Maxwell.' She ignored Jane. 'You're earlier than I expected. I'll examine your wife here and see if it is worth giving her a room.' She deigned to notice Jane. 'Are your pains coming regularly, Mrs Maxwell?'

'Yes, more or less.'

'More or less, she says. Doctor?' She looked at him.

50

'Her membranes have ruptured, matron.' He wasn't clear if that effected the regularity or irregularity of the pains.

'Well, we'll have a look. Lie still, Mrs Maxwell.' Her top half disappeared up Jane's white gown. After a minute or so she reappeared.

'No presentation yet, doctor. I'm afraid it will be some time. There's no purpose in you hanging on.'

'I can wait . . .'

'No, I don't like men cluttering up my birthing room, doctor or no doctor. You'll be in good hands,' she said to Jane. There was no reassuring smile. 'Now, if you'll excuse me, I have other patients to attend to.' She went out with the same composure as she had entered.

They looked at each other. 'You had better get off,' Jane said. There were tears in her eyes.

'I hate leaving you.'

'It could be ages, and there's no one to answer the door or the tube. Someone's bound to use it.' They still jumped when they heard a strange voice circling their bedroom. 'And I can only do this alone.' She smiled, and bit her lip. Someone knocked and the young nurse they had seen earlier came in.

'Matron wants me to take down Mrs Maxwell's particulars,' she said, looking pointedly at John. He nodded and bent over Jane, lying pole-axed on the high bed.

'I suppose I should get away.' He kissed her. 'I wonder if all men feel as awful as I do at this stage?'

'Possibly.' She was stern, and seemed anxious to get rid of him. 'Yes, on you go, darling. I'll be all right.' A spasm of pain crossed her face and he held her hands tightly until it passed.

51

He heard the nurse coughing. You haven't any idea how it feels, he thought, to watch your wife in agony because of your own pleasure – well, both of us. He laid his hand on Jane's cheek, then walked to the door. He waved and went out.

He tortured himself all the way home. Her agony, a first baby, dry labour and that frustrated old maid of a matron. And then he thought of the coming baby, theirs, and how they had always presumed they'd have a family. And yet, to be perfectly honest, he was experiencing a feeling of relief at having been told to clear out and leave it to others. He'd just have been a nuisance.

The house seemed gloomier and emptier when he got back. He was going up the dark staircase when he heard the ghostly voice from the bedroom. 'Doctor, doctor, me mam's right bad. I think it's coming . . .' He groaned and went to fetch his bag.

Jane watched John's retreating back as he seemed to slink out of the room. The words occurred to her: 'A nice stew we've landed ourselves in.' Anyhow it was over to her now. She met the matron's reproving look bent on her, seeming to echo her thoughts.

Don't make such a fuss, the look seemed to say as a loud yell escaped her. 'The girl who was here before you had twins, easy as pie.'

'She was lucky,' Jane panted. 'No one told me it would be like this.'

'Do you hear that, nurse?' the matron said.

The nurse, a young girl with untidy hair escaping from her cap, looked compassionately at Jane. 'Perhaps she hasn't a mother, matron.'

'My mother died suddenly a while ago.' She was

haughty as she spoke and then dissolved into tears, sniffing, wiping her nose on the sleeve of the gown. There was no place in it for a handkerchief. She was aware of the silence of the two women, and a kind of sound from the matron, 'Tchk, tchk.'

'Well, we'd better get on with it,' the woman said, as if she was involved. 'Push! Call that a push, put your heart into it, Mrs Maxwell, that's better, push! You've been spoiled. Most of the girls who come in here have worked on farms or in munitions. And you have a doctor for a husband. Didn't he give you any information about what to expect, or didn't he know?' Jane turned her head away from the baleful stare bent upon her. 'Keep an eye on her, nurse,' the matron said. 'I have to go next door to see how Mrs Tait is doing.'

When she had left the room Jane met the nurse's friendly look. 'Don't worry about her. She never had any children herself, and she doesn't really approve of the whole business. I'm sorry you lost your ma, dear. Men don't realize, doctor or no doctor. Let your body take over, it'll tell you when to push.'

'It's like being in a bloody vice,' Jane said.

'You're right there. I'll have a look.' She disappeared then bobbed up again. 'The head's showing. A good push now should do it. Keep it up. We'll give matron a surprise when she comes back.'

The girl gave Jane confidence. She bore down, pushed, yelled, swore, words which she didn't realize she knew. No one had warned her. If she'd had a friend . . . but with coming to Tynebay, there had been none, and John had never given her any information. There ought to be classes, she thought. Or they should let your husband stay with you to hold your hand, or at least see what you had been let in for. Then, poor John, she thought, he'll be suffering for me. Perhaps he'll be thinking we were silly to have a baby when there was a war on.

And then, suddenly, amidst the pain and the yelling, she found a baby wrapped in a shawl in her arm, and she was looking down on a face which didn't seem to look like her or John, a little old face with small hands clutching at air, and moving its head towards her breast.

'You've done it, love,' the nurse said. 'A boy, a lovely little boy, with a fine pair of lungs.' The baby opened its mouth and demonstrated its fine pair of lungs, then turned towards Jane's breast again. 'We'll have to get you stitched, though, you're badly torn.'

The matron's face was there again, frowning, not beaming down on her. 'Your husband will be pleased. Men always like a boy first. I'll get the doctor to come in and stitch you up. He's with the other patient next door. She's got a girl.'

Jane felt immediate pride. Never again, she thought. A boy should please John. Never again.

The doctor who came into the room congratulated her on the birth of a baby boy. It seemed she had done the right thing. After he had finished with her, she was taken into a ward with several women in it, who greeted her with smiles and congratulations. There were various comments about 'The Dragon' and one of the women said, 'You haven't finished with her yet, there's the castor oil to come!' They all groaned and commented in their Newcastle voices, which were still strange to Jane's ears.

'Nurse, nurse, I'm getting *warse*,' she heard one woman call out, and the young nurse, hair untidier than ever, came in and reprimanded them. 'You're like a crowd of naughty children,' she told them. 'Mrs Maxwell is from Tynebay and her husband is a doctor, so behave yourselves.' Jane wondered what had happened to the room John had booked, but felt quite glad of the moral support in the ward.

Five

J ane lay in bed the following morning in the ward of
the Northcliffe Nursing Home, listening to the rum-
blings in her stomach. She saw two people standing at the
entrance to the ward, looking around. One was Dr Moir,
the other a woman. A nurse was indicating Jane's bed,
and she watched the couple come towards her. The
woman was in a red suit, with a floating scarf, and as
she drew nearer, Jane was reminded of a Modigliani
drawing she had once seen, the white face, pointed chin
and black hair. They stopped at her bedside.

'My wife wanted to come and see you, Mrs Maxwell,'
Dr Moir said, as if he had been dragooned.

'It's good of you to come. Please sit down.' She
indicated two seats.

Mrs Moir laid a bunch of dahlias on Jane's counterpane. 'I'm sorry. There was nothing in the garden but
those, end of summer, I'm afraid. We live in Belsay, quite
near here, and I thought if Charles stopped on his way to
the practice, I could visit you. How are you feeling?'

'Fine, thank you, Mrs Moir,' Jane said. Her stomach
rumbled ominously, and she put her hand on it. 'The
matron here has decided views. She gives each mother a
spoonful of castor oil after the baby is born. I'm suffering
from that now.'

56

'That's a stupid practice, isn't it, Charles?' Mrs Moir said.

He looked down his nose. 'The matron here is very reliable. I always recommend her.'

Mrs Moir made a slight grimace. 'How ridiculous!' She turned to Jane. 'May I look at your baby?' The cot was at the side of Jane's bed.

'Yes, please do.' She watched the woman bend over Scott's cot. Her face was now that of a Madonna's, tender, and sad.

'He's absolutely adorable!' She made a curious downward gesture with her hand as if she was brushing somebody or something away. 'I didn't think children would be allowed in,' she said.

'Oh, they're not! It's because of infection, I suppose.' Jane was puzzled. She looked at Dr Moir and he met her enquiring look with a fixed gaze.

'I'll tell your husband I've seen you and that you're looking fine,' he said. It was as if he hadn't heard his wife's remark. 'I'm hoping to keep him. I have a friend who is a councillor, and he told me that we were short of doctors in this area, and he had every confidence that Dr Maxwell would be left here.'

'Is that James Anderson?' Mrs Moir said, flinging her scarf round her throat. 'I met his wife yesterday, and she said that they were getting ready to go to Spain. He's retired now.'

Her husband looked annoyed. 'He told me it would be all right. He knows the trouble I've had with doctors.'

'Yes, Charles has had a terrible time,' Mrs Moir said to Jane. 'You can't imagine . . . How do you like your house, Mrs Maxwell?' She abruptly changed the subject.

'It's nice to have a place of our own, although the speaking tube is a bit of a nuisance!' Jane laughed.

'Don't I know it! Do you remember, Charles? It was our first home too, and then my father bought our house in Belsay for us, after . . . well, I'm not supposed to speak of it.'

'I'm sure Mrs Maxwell doesn't want to hear our history, Stella,' Dr Moir said.

'What's the food like here?' Mrs Moir seemed to fire the question.

It caused Jane to remember the meal she'd had last night, steak and kidney pie, vegetables, everything swamped in thick gluey gravy. Her stomach rumbled loudly. She felt suddenly acutely nauseated by the stabs of pain, like hands kneading it. What am I going to do, she thought, with these two people. They're so peculiar. I could have told anyone else. She saw a nurse walking down the corridor between beds, and beckoned her. When she came to her, Jane raised an anguished face, put her hand on her stomach, and the nurse fortunately understood. She nodded and went quickly back up the ward.

'I'm afraid I'm going to have to ask you to go to the waiting room for a few minutes,' Jane said.

'Well, of course,' Mrs Moir got up. 'Come along, Charles. We'll come back. I want to have a nice chat with you. We must get to know each other . . .'

'I'll push along,' Dr Moir said. 'I'll tell your husband we've seen you.'

'Tell him I'm dying to see him,' Jane said, and saw a look of distaste pass over his face.

'There will be a big list for him today, because of me looking in here,' he said, 'but I'll tell him.'

58

The nurse appeared with a bedpan concealed by a white cloth. She looked at the Moirs and said, 'The waiting room is at the foot of the ward.' Mr and Mrs Moir retreated up the corridor.

'It's that castor oil,' Jane said to the nurse, who was the one who had attended to her during Scott's birth.

'Yes, I know. As if you hadn't suffered enough. Here you are, then.'

From her seat on the bedpan Jane watched the Moirs at the top of the ward. They were walking slightly apart. She and John clasped hands, or some-times he put an arm round her. 'What bliss,' she whispered, thinking of the relief, and John at the same time. 'What utter bliss!'

She was ready to receive Mrs Moir when she came back. 'Charles fusses about the practice so much,' the woman said. 'Now we can have that nice little chat.'

'How will you get back?' Jane said, wishing she could lie down and close her eyes.

'By bus, or I can get a taxi at the bus stop. Don't worry about me. Charles doesn't. Oh, I do hope you can stay on in the practice.'

Jane decided not to say anything. She felt it might be repeated to Dr Moir. 'I'm sorry I had to rush you away. But that castor oil!'

'Charles likes this place. I believe he recommended it to your husband. But the matron is known to be a perfect dragon. I'm glad I never had to have any dealings with her.'

'Do you have any children, Mrs Moir?' Jane asked her. An odd look crossed the woman's face.

'A girl, Lucy, but she died at birth. You can under-stand why I don't like it here . . . but I said to Charles, I must not dwell on losing Lucy, I'll go and see Mrs Maxwell. You're just a girl, aren't you?'

'I've always looked younger than my age. I'm twenty-five.'

She looked at Mrs Moir, and saw the woman was smiling as she had done before, her gaze shifting downwards. A peculiar indulgent smile. 'They follow you everywhere, don't they?' she looked up at Jane.

'I don't understand,' Jane said. 'Who?'

'*You* know.' Mrs Moir patted Jane's arm. 'You'll find that with your little boy. Whether he is with you or not, you won't be able to forget him. Charles doesn't understand.'

'I think I do. After all, you've had a baby in you for nine months, and there is a link which perhaps husbands don't feel.'

'How understanding you are! I think you and I are going to be good friends. Shall I tell you about my plan?' Jane nodded. 'Well, I've got some money saved up, from my housekeeping allowance. I'm going to buy a car, and keep it somewhere in the village, without telling Charles, then when he's away at the practice, I can go anywhere I like. I'll pick you up, and you will have to warn me if he's there, and we'll go to the cinema in Newcastle, and have afternoon tea in a café I know in Gray Street. I love it, that sweep. Or, if it's a good day, we'll drive into the country. Northumberland has some lovely country. Not many people realize that.'

'That sounds very nice.' She's weird, Jane thought. Is she the reason for Dr Moir's forbidding exterior? He won't be able to take her anywhere because of her odd remarks.

'And you can come and have tea with me, and see your old house,' Jane said.

'Oh, I shouldn't like that. That place has nothing but unpleasant memories for me.'

'Were you there when your little girl was born?'

'What little girl?'

'The one you told me about.'

'Oh, Lucy!' She laughed, throwing her scarf over her shoulder. 'She doesn't really exist. That's what Charles says, so I have to believe him.'

The nurse was at Jane's bedside. 'Visitors have to leave now,' she said, looking at Mrs Moir.

'Me! Of course. What's on the menu today, nurse?'

The nurse looked at Jane, her eyebrows raised, and said, 'Pork and vegetables, cauliflower, potatoes, rice pudding.'

'Well, remember to treat Mrs Maxwell well. Her husband is Dr Moir's partner, and nothing but the best is good enough for her.'

'We'll do that, Mrs Moir.'

Jane watched Mrs Moir walking down the corridor, bowing at intervals to the occupants of other beds. She met the nurse's eyes. 'I'll get your lunch now.'

'Please, less vegetables, nurse. The caster oil has made me feel queasy.'

'Or maybe having visitors too early.' She gave Jane an enigmatic smile, and left.

If the Moirs had been too early, John was too late. Jane saw him at the entrance talking to a nurse. Everybody was bedded down, the lights lowered, and she had been given a glass of Horlicks which she hadn't drunk. She waved to him, and he came quickly towards her.

'I had to persuade the nurse to let me in. How are you, darling?' He bent over her and kissed her.

'Fine. Waiting for you.'

'Where's the baby?'

'They remove them to allow us to sleep. Ask to see him on your way out. Did Dr Moir tell you he had visited me with his wife?'

'Yes, and he gave me a list as long as my arm and some vaccinations to do. I didn't make myself any supper. I just drove here as soon as I could.'

'Oh, John! You need me to look after you. What a funny pair the Moirs are! He didn't unbend. He had brought his wife at her request, and she did all the talking. She's funny, John, I wonder if that's why he looks so miserable most of the time.'

'Do you mean funny-peculiar, or funny-ha-ha?'

'Odd. You begin to think you're imagining things. She seems to see her little girl, Lucy. But she's dead.'

'Goodness! That was upsetting.'

'Yes, I felt nauseated, not because of her, and had to ask the nurse to get me a bedpan. They give you castor oil here after giving birth.'

'Whose idea was that?'

'The matron's.' She looked at him. 'What's happened to you? You look pale.'

'Do I? The worst. I've got my call-up papers.'

'Oh, no!' She held out her arms to him, and he bent over her and they kissed. 'That's terrible. Have you told Dr Moir?'

'Yes, but he took it very badly. Said it couldn't be true, that he had arranged that I wouldn't be. And that was why he had given me the partnership.'

'Well, it's not your fault.'

'No, but he's acting as if it were. Went past me during the day with a set face.'

'His wife warned him about a councillor who had been

looking after his interests, but was now retiring. I could see he didn't believe her. How long have we got, John?'

'A fortnight.' She saw his eyes. He was excited at the prospect, as she had known he would be.

'I'll tell the matron I'm leaving in a day or so.'

'See how you feel, darling. But it would be nice if you were back home with the baby before I have to go.'

'Oh, dear!' She fought back the tears, and he stroked her face. 'I'm not going to cry,' she said. 'We'll discuss it when I'm back home. Tell me how much you love me.'

'I love you. You tell me.'

She held the tears back until he had gone, then lay down and pulled the bedclothes over her face, in case the other girls should see her weeping.

Six

1971

The next day after Boris visited was still hot, and it was late afternoon before Jane set out to walk to St. Martin to shop there. It was the right time. The shopkeepers took a two-hour break, and seemed to get a new lease of life around four o'clock. The villagers emerged with their baskets; Madame Gitang took off the green net covers from her outdoor display of vegetables and fruit; Monsieur Gaillard, *le bouchier*, set out his wooden board advertizing all his choicest cuts; Madame Desirée, Monsieur Gaillard's wife – John had said there was a lot to desire in her buxom figure and short-sleeved white coat, showing her plump arms – generally stood in the doorway welcoming their customers. The children out of school played tag around the war memorial with its stone celtic cross poised above it.

The names on the memorial were village names, a dozen or two, and there were a few of them – those who had survived the two wars – buried in the cemetery just outside the village at the crossroads. A peaceful place with the same peaceful view as Jane had from her own cottage.

When she was passing Monsieur Graf's house she saw Boris talking to a small group of people seated on

deckchairs in the front garden. There was a perambulator beside them in which she could just see the form of a
small sleeping baby. The new people, she thought, and
would have carried on but Boris hailed her.

'*Bonne chance*, Jane! Come and meet our new neighbours!' She hesitated, smiling, and then went towards
them.

Boris put his arm round her. 'Come along now.
Don't be shy. This is Mr Graf's nephew and wife
and daughter and little granddaughter. Jane Maxwell.
She's in that delightful cottage above you.' He gestured
with his head.

The man rose and held out his hand, the two women
remained seated, smiling up at her. 'I'm Jan Graf,' he
said. 'This is my wife, Bella, and daughter, Rose.' The
women held out their hands, moving as if to rise.

'Please don't get up!' Jane said. Mrs Graf was black-
haired, plumply pretty; the daughter, flaxen fair, more
like her father, who was fair-skinned and handsome.

'And there's my baby too, Rosabel!' The young woman was now on her feet, beaming with pride, and
bending over the perambulator, pulling back the covers
to show a tiny baby, fair also, shell-pink complexioned.
The eyelashes swept the round little cheeks. The child
had an air of fragility.

'She's adorable,' Jane said, bending also. Scott had
been like that once. 'How old is she?'

'Three months. She was premature, and I wasn't too
well, so my poor husband is working to make up for the
time he took off when I was in hospital. Father and
Mother persuaded me to come with them for a little
holiday.'

Mr Graf pushed forward a chair for Jane. 'You must

sit down and let us get to know each other. Mr Halliwell has just joined us.'

'Just for a moment, then. I'm walking to St. Martin to do some shopping.'

'Isn't it too hot for you?' Bella Graf said. 'If I were you, I should have driven.'

Jane sat down beside her. 'I don't have a car. I gave up driving some years ago.' She still felt the small nagging pain above her ribs if the subject came up. Surely by this time . . .

'We'll have a drink and I shall drive you,' Jan Graf said decidedly.

'Well . . .'

'You'll find Jane a stubborn lady,' Boris said.

'I'm particularly persuasive with stubborn ladies.' The other man smiled at Jane, a smile which deliberately locked her eyes for a second. Her hidden hackles rose but she turned to his wife, subduing the feeling.

'How do you like Laborie, Madame Graf?'

'Quite charming. My uncle-in-law was very attached to it. I already feel the same and we only arrived last evening.'

'It had the same effect on Jane and me,' Boris said, 'and also John, her husband.'

'Isn't he here?' Bella Graf turned to Jane.

'He . . . died.' She still found it difficult to say. Boris' eyes were kind.

'My wife, Hazel, is the only dissenter,' he said. 'Prefers London. Thinks all this is . . . bucolic.'

'So I've arrived just at the right time!' Jan Graf was standing beside them with a tray of drinks. 'My special concoction, June Delight, I call it.'

'If it's like Papa's usual mixtures,' his daughter said, 'I

guarantee you'll succumb to being driven to St. Martin willingly.' There was general laughter, but when Jane met Bella Graf's eyes she thought they didn't match her smile, which was practised, but without warmth.

The drink was certainly potent. They quickly became at ease with each other. The day was languorous; Jane felt they were interesting people who would make good neighbours, easy to get on with. Boris was at his most amusing, and they laughed and talked whilst the sun shone down golden on the small party, seeming to Jane to edge it with a rim of gold, dream-like. She felt as if she were hovering above it, like a bird, observing it. The talk was broken up by a piercing little cry from the baby.

'Ah, my little pet!' Bella Graf made a move to rise from her chair.

'Mama, stay where you are!' Rose was on her feet already, flushed and pretty. 'What the little pet wants is something you can't give her.' There was general laughter, but Jane thought the tone of Rose's voice was slightly acerbic.

'I must go.' Jane got up. 'I shall be walking on air to St. Martin. It's been lovely meeting you all.'

Jan Graf was on his feet also. 'My car is at your disposal. I shall be very disappointed if you don't allow me . . .'

'It's too good of you, but I enjoy the walk,' Jane insisted.

'You must respect Jane's wishes, Jan,' Bella said, then turned to Jane. 'I insist you join us for dinner as a recompense. I prepared it all this morning and put it in the refrigerator.'

'Do let Mama show off her prowess.' Rose had the baby in her arms, and Jane went to peep at the child. Was

67

she imagining a hidden frisson between mother and daughter? Anyhow it would be ungracious if she refused.

'Thank you so much. I'd be delighted.'

'As a further inducement,' Boris said, 'I have already been invited to join the party.' His grin convinced her.

'What time would you like me, Madame Graf?'

'Bella, please, I've already taken the liberty of calling you Jane,' she said in a decided tone, as if it was a tactic she had used before. 'Come at eight.'

Jane smiled in acquiescence. '*Au revoir*. I'll see you all at eight. Thank you so much.'

She walked quickly downhill, turned into the rough road which led to St. Martin, in between fields where the fat cows grazed, past the cemetery with its high wall and impressive gates, up to the crossroads at the post office, thinking, he didn't press me after all to accept a lift. Was it because of his wife? Don't say you're disappointed, Jane, she told herself. The post office was shut and she had wanted stamps. That was the reason for her disappointment, of course.

Nevertheless, in the ten minutes' walk her mind had been full of the new arrivals. Mr Graf's handsome nephew, assured, possibly early fifties, his pretty wife younger but with older eyes, the young girl flushed with pride of motherhood, but perhaps a little suspicious of her mother's proprietorial claims on the baby as all new young mothers were, and the final impression, the fragility of the small baby with the large blue eyes above the small roseleaf cheeks.

Scott had had blue eyes at the beginning, large, dark-lashed, but they had changed colour when he was older to the brown eyes of his father. 'You shouldn't miss John with eyes like that!' people had said, but Scott's eyes had something lacking in them compared with John's, that spirited quality of his, a hint of bravado, of devil-may-care. Scott's were steady, and almost haughty. Did all only children feel that the world spun round them?

Oh, but he had been beguiling, her John. Only hers? She felt the shadow again, dismissed it. Think rather of that sweet baby today, of Scott as a baby, with Scottish parents but born in a cold north-eastern town in England in the early years of the war . . .

Seven

The weather changed overnight. Jane had found this out during the many years they had spent on holiday at Laborie, its complete breakdown after a period of excessive heat.

There was torrential rain, thunder and lightning. Sometimes they had treated it as an entertainment, Scott, John and herself, sitting under the inadequate shelter of the roof of the *bolet*, wearing raincoats, and holding up umbrellas to catch the drips, enjoying the 3-D spectacle of the lightning racing like a searchlight over the landscape, weirdly illuminating it, the staccato cymbal-like peals of thunder. She could almost see Scott's face, his clapping hands. 'A good one, oh, Dad, a good one!'

Madame Lisieux always warned them about the electricity. 'Please, dear Madame, remove the plug of the television. *C'est très dangereux.*' Once they had omitted to do this, and the television had been a small spectacle on its own with flashes and bangs and explosions. They had been obliged to go to Gramon the next day and shamefully replace it so as not to incur Madame's wrath, or at least her extreme disappointment in their non-comprehension of the vagaries of the French electricity system.

As John had said, 'Why on earth was it so unreliable

70

when the mighty Dordogne had hydro-electric stations every hundred yards?'

But this bout of bad weather gave her no excuse. She would get down to writing. 'Getting down to' described the state very well, for once she had got used to the small Olivetti she'd always owned – computers or even electric typewriters were out of the question – she descended into the past, and more importantly, deep inside herself.

As she tapped, slowly because of her inexpertise, digging painfully, because she was, in a way, like a miner, except that she was searching for truth, not coal or tin, she began to see the panorama of her past life, not as she had lived it but retrospectively and highlit here and there in all its shades of meaning and implications.

It was a slow progress, and at the end of a day, she had changed most of what she had written. But as the thunder and lightning went, and the rain settled into a solid downpour, she began to feel a newly-discovered sense, an appreciation, an awareness of all the times when her thinking had been wrong, as had been her attitudes and behaviour. Only in retrospect, and with her painfully acquired wisdom, could she begin to see her faults.

Her greatest regret was what she now saw as her self-absorption, her failure to see events from John's point of view, her failure to appreciate his essential sweetness, his lack of malice, and his ever-present Peter Pannish sense of fun. Her critical faculties had always been too acute, very seldom did anyone get the benefit of doubt, and as time went on this had developed into a kind of cynicism. As with the Cains. 'They're taking advantage of you.' And the bitterness she felt towards Mrs Cain who had called him out on that freezing night, because

71

her husband had had a heart attack. The dog it was that died. Mr Cain had recovered, but John had died as a result of a cold he had got that night which had settled on his lungs.

She tried to console herself. Surely in those early years she had been loving, had always supported him, surely she had been brave when he was called up, as they had always known he would be. Stoicism had been her strong point. She had turned away from offers of comfort from his parents, nor had she offered much to them. She could have been more of a loving daughter-in-law, a stronger support, could have better recognized that their anxiety was as great as her own.

Wouldn't it, she thought now, have been better to have been less brave, to let Scott see, not an always smiling face, but someone who grieved for a lover and a father? That was her role during the war, she had thought, to fill in for John. Although Scott had been too young to understand that, as he grew out of babyhood, had her attitude resulted in him having no sense of loss of a father figure? With stoicism there was little room for tenderness.

Scott had got all her love when John was away. All that love which had been meant for John had poured over him. The war must have been for him a sunny paradise of love, bathing only him.

She sat motionless more often in front of the typewriter than using it. As the rain cleared and the strong sun reasserted itself, she began to think of mundane things, that Friday was the day of the fish market in Gramon, that she needed milk and eggs from the farm, and that she should telephone for a taxi.

And she thought of her neighbours. It was strange that

Boris hadn't driven up to see if she were all right. And what about the Graf family? How were they getting on, and that sweet baby. How fragile it had looked. Scott had never been fragile. From the early days, admirers peeping into his pram had no trouble with his gender. 'What a fine little boy!' they had said.

Gramon was busy as it always was on market days. The streets were thronged with people around the stalls, the traffic was banished for the day. The same cotton dresses were on sale for farmers' wives, black background, small white print, the same swarthy-skinned salesmen wooed the women with their trinkets. The sad-eyed Indian with the carved wooden toys sat at his stall alone. Even country children preferred the gaudy plastic ones which broke before they got them home. And hens clucked noisily in their coops.

Jane went to the patisserie to get some of her favourite *choux* cream cakes. They were a special treat to herself to remind her of former times when she had bought them for John, who'd had a sweet tooth. She promised herself one after her meal tonight.

She climbed the steep narrow Rue De l'Horloge to the castle where the fish market had staked out its territory, and marvelled again at the choice of fish and crustaceans in a place so far removed from the sea.

She felt strangely lonely today amidst the bustle. When she had made her purchases, she went back down the little street, not stopping to admire Madame Léonie's dresses, nor the handmade jewellery in the little shop where the young man sat, bowed over his bench. Instead she made for René's café, where she had decided to have a drink. The waiter greeted her like an old friend, which she was.

73

'*Bonjour, madame. Enfin, c'est bon! Quel mauvais temps, n'est-ce-pas?*' She imagined sympathy in his eyes. He would well remember she and John coming here most mornings on their settled little routine of shopping, buying an English paper, finishing with a *cassis*. Scott had deserted them when he left school for university, preferring more exciting trips with friends.

There were plenty of people around her, plenty of chatter, but no one she knew. She had felt more at home in the shops where she was an old and valued customer, but here she felt a nagging little doubt, possibly for the first time. Had she done the right thing in coming back to Laborie? What would it be like when she became really old if she had to rely on strange medical care, and wouldn't she long for the comfort of hearing her own tongue being spoken? Was there enough mental stimulus here? The excessive politeness of the local people . . . didn't it hide the lack of what she called *real* conversation?

You're gloomy, she told herself. There's Boris and Hazel, and there's the new family, and you used to sit and chat with Madame Lamartine, whose remarks about the villagers at St. Martin, where she had been brought up, always amused you. And you promised yourself you would investigate the societies at Gramon. After all, they have a music festival every year. And you could spend a day at Cahors from time to time, even go to the cinema . . . but, no, you haven't a car. You gave up driving. The almost forgotten nagging ache was there again under her ribs, the guilt.

She went inside to the bar and telephoned for a taxi. René, the owner, greeted her with seeming pleasure. She was cheerful again, and she stayed chatting with him until Richard, the taxi man, appeared at the door.

She listened on the way back to his tales about the prowess of his children, at least two of them. The third, Berthe, was '*assez aimable*', he said with a heavy sigh.

'She'll probably surprise you yet,' Jane said.

'*Peut-être*. She can always get married,' he said, as if it was the best he could hope for. She thought of her own brilliant career nipped in the bud when she married John. At least she liked to tell herself that, although efficient and personable, she hadn't been in love with the business world. She lacked the hard edge of the successful career woman.

She noticed, as they drove through the hamlet, that neither Boris nor the Grafs were to be seen, but it didn't worry her unduly. Everyone had their own plans and engagements. She was quite self-sufficient, she told herself, otherwise she wouldn't have contemplated coming here in the first place. She passed the brick-built *lavoir* where the Laborie women used to wash their clothes, as Madame Lamartine had told her. If she had lived then there would have been little time for dreaming or speculation.

There was the small joy of putting away her purchases, preparing her meal, and she was having her coffee outside when a car drove up swiftly, turned with rather a dash, and stopped beside her. Jan Graf got out. 'Good evening,' he said, coming towards her over the grass, and quaintly, bowing. 'Am I intruding on your privacy?'

'Not at all. Come and join me.' She indicated one of the wooden garden chairs beside her.

'Thank you.' He sat down.

'Would you like a drink?' she asked. 'I'll go upstairs and get—'

He interrupted her, 'It's too much trouble . . .'

'Well, if you think that,' she smiled, 'they're all on the sideboard in the kitchen. Go and help yourself. And bring one for me also. There's some Pineau there.'

'*Bonne idée.* I can't resist!' He was gone, and she saw how he went up the *bolet* steps with a lithe swiftness.

There was a lionlike quality about him, because of his colouring, and the smoothness of his movements. He was back in no time with the bottle and two glasses. He poured with skill, handed her a glass, and sat down again beside her.

'I was lonely, and I thought, that nice Mrs Maxwell will take pity on me.' She laughed. 'Have I said something to amuse you?' he asked.

'No, not really, but the way you said "Mrs Maxwell" reminded me that my husband's patients in England called me "Mrs Doctor Maxwell". I can't think why it came to me, really . . .' She looked away.

'You must miss your husband.'

'Yes.'

'And so you decided to come here. That surprises me.'

'It surprised quite a few people, but we always loved it. There are two schools of thought, I notice. One group thinks it would hurt too much to go back, the other group thinks it wise.'

'And you evidently belong to the second category?'

'That's it.' She didn't want to talk about herself, tell him what her chief reason was. She changed the subject. 'Do you know where Boris has got to?'

'Yes, he went off to Toulouse for a few days with his wife. She arrived when the rain came. I think they've gone to look for fittings for the house.'

'Oh, good! Perhaps Hazel is beginning to look forward to it after all.'

'It's an excuse to shop. I believe she likes city life.' He gave her a smiling glance as if they both understood Hazel. 'As for me, my wife, daughter and little Rosabel have returned to Amsterdam.'

Jane was surprised. 'But they've only just come!'

'I know, but Bella's a very determined lady. The baby was running a little temperature, they visited the doctor at Gramon, and he suggested they see their own specialist back in Holland. Or Bella suggested it to him. Grandmothers are fussier about their grandchildren than their own.'

'I wouldn't know. Well, perhaps it's wise, since the baby was premature, wasn't she?'

'Yes.' He was examining his glass, twirling it between his fingers and he suddenly looked up at her. 'I wondered if you would take pity on a lonely man and let me take you out to dinner?'

'Well . . .' She wasn't sure. What would the forceful Bella think?

'Do say yes. The last few days have been awful for me with the dreadful weather. I have only plans for a limited stay, and I haven't brought any work to keep me busy.'

'You're a workaholic?'

'A bit. I was advised to have a month off. So you don't find the time difficult to fill in?'

'No.' She shook her head. 'I've come to write, actually.' She gave a shamefaced little laugh.

'A kind of therapy?'

'I never thought of it as that. Rather an exploration. I had a very busy life. I never had time.'

'And it had to be here?' He smiled at her again. 'Look, I won't be deflected. Are you going to be kind and have dinner with me and we can have a nice metaphysical conversation while we eat?'

She met his glance. At fifty-four, she thought, I can't say, 'Wouldn't your wife not mind?' Surely she was more sophisticated than that. 'Yes,' she said, 'thank you. I would like that very much.'

Eight

They had established a good rapport over the wine when they set off for the Pont l'Isle, so full of memories for Jane, up hill and down dale, through the village where the dogs barked at every passing car, probably because there were so few. Then there was the village where she and John had stopped, because he had spotted a grass snake slithering through the bank at the roadside. When they had got out, she had crouched down to examine it, and had been captivated by its shining and beautifully marked skin, reminding her, she said teasingly, of the matching shoes and handbag she had seen in a certain exclusive shop in Glasgow's Sauchiehall Street. How many snakeskins would it take, she had asked him, and wasn't it sad to think of those beautiful reptiles desecrated in such a fashion. 'What a gruesome little mind you have!' he had laughed at her.

When she and Jan got to the restaurant, they found it busy, especially the main dining area which was situated outside, under an awning, and lit by golden, globelike lamps. There was a buzz of conversation backed by the tinkle of a piano. A man in evening clothes was playing. 'How trite,' she wanted to say. Fortunately they found a vacant table in a trellised corner overlooking the river, which they both agreed was a better choice.

'It's nice to hear the water,' Jane said, and Jan agreed, saying he could see a waterfall from his seat.

She and John had celebrated her birthday here; it must have been her fortieth, she thought, because Scott had been spending that holiday with a school friend, and when they got back to the cottage, they had made love, not in the juvenile, excitable way they had at the mental hospital, but more mature, and no less loving. He had said, 'When I think of those lonely nights in Burma, where I missed you so much!' she had felt pity at the time, for him. It had been a lovely evening. She remembered driving back with a huge moon half-hidden behind the trees. The memory was only spoiled later.

She and Jan chose the menu together: *foie gras, ris de veau* with *morelles* and *pommes dauphines*, the sweet to be chosen later, perhaps cheese. They both confessed to a love of the local *chèvre*.

'Splendid menu,' Jan said. 'The chef isn't above introducing country fare.' He called the waiter, and ordered a bottle of champagne. When she protested, he said, 'Do you like it?' She confessed she did, on occasions, and he said, 'Regard this as an occasion.'

He went on: 'When I was young, my father used to take the whole family, and our mother, of course, to the Krasnapolsky Hotel in Amsterdam, for Sunday lunch. Do you know Amsterdam?'

'No. France was always our destination.'

'It's in the hub of the city, Dam Square, opposite the Royal Palace. It was very much a custom amongst certain families, this Sunday visit. The women chattered, the children played together, and the chef produced a special menu for them. It was there that I met Bella for the first time. She would be fourteen, with dark ringlets

and rosy cheeks, and I would be two years older. There-
after I met her at parties given by neighbouring families,
and balls, generally at the Krasnapolsky. It was a little
world.'

How lucky John and I were to meet, Jane thought, no
family backing like that. 'John and I were too young
when we married,' she told him. 'I often think we weren't
sophisticated enough about life. I had been anxious to
get away from home, he came along at the right time, and
he . . .' She was going to say 'was very passionate'. 'Well,
the morals of the time made it necessary to be married to
enjoy each other. Do you understand?'

'Completely. I heard marriage referred to at that time
as "married concubinage". The mores of the time de-
creed it. Holland, perhaps, advanced at a greater rate
than England. You didn't shake yourself free until the
sixties, then your children did it for you.'

She nodded. 'We took a leaf out of their book, and
began to think we were missing something. John and I
were never in such an environment, but we heard about
parties where wife-swapping was all the rage. How did
we get on to this subject?' She laughed.

'Sex?' he said.

She took a sip from her champagne glass, trying to
look sophisticated. Actually, she thought, we wouldn't
have gone to such parties. We were too much in love.

'You look wistful,' Jan said.

'Memories,' she said. 'You can't put old heads on
young shoulders.'

'Would you change things if you could?'

She thought for a minute. 'I don't think I would. I
realize now I missed out on a lot of the so-called fun,
possibly because of the war, and my inability to move

with the times.' She thought of that dull room in Tynebay, of dancing with Roger Mills, the temporary assistant who had replaced John.

'You can get mesmerized by fun and romance. I did.
Bella was always in my mind associated with the Krasnapolsky, the elegant background, pillars and flights of
steps, white linen-covered tables, flowers, waiters flitting
about. The excitement of going there, knowing I would
see her, being driven up to the entrance by my father in
his old sedan, with my young sister sitting on my knee,
giggling and being reprimanded by Mama, and Father
handing over the keys of the car to the commissionaire,
so that he could park it properly, and my heart beating at
the thought of seeing Bella again. Pure romance, not
love.'

'Do you regret it?'

'No, just that you realize you fell in love with someone
who didn't exist, and then when you married . . .'

They sat for a long time over their coffee, listening to
the rippling of the river, the background of the piano
with its Twenties tunes, and the chatter of voices. They
didn't speak much, as if they both knew they had been
indiscreet.

Sometimes when Jane raised her eyes she found Jan's
on her. To cover her confusion, she shivered a little, and
he said immediately, 'Do you find it cold?'

'A little,' she said.

'Shall we go now?'

'Perhaps we'd better.'

'There's no one spying on us.'

She laughed. 'No, there's no one spying on us,' she
said.

She went to the ladies' room while he was paying the

bill, and her face in the mirror looked rosy, the eyes dark yet lit up, as if with excitement. Has our conversation been too pointed, she wondered.

Nevertheless, she felt they had established a good rapport when they set off. She didn't have to make conversation, she could let her thoughts roam. The visit to the Pont l'Isle had been full of memories for her, now once again they were driving up hill and down dale. She heard Jan's voice. 'I hope going to that place didn't make you miss your husband even more. You looked so wistful at times.'

'It's strange, John used to say the same thing about me. To tell you the truth, I think I was a bit childish. You see, I had a dull life before I met him, and when he came along it was like a prince riding by. He introduced me to a new life, laughter and love, which I had never known, it was such a release for me. We laughed and loved and were very happy, until he went away to the war and I was left with our son to bring up. When he came home on leave, that, I think, was when he said I looked wistful. He, on the other hand, looked happy, he couldn't disguise it.'

John never drove like this, she thought, you could read a person by their driving. Jan seemed to whizz round corners as if they were a challenge. With John she had felt utterly safe, which was how she had always felt with him, protected. She should have remembered that . . .

'I think you and I possibly made the same mistake,' Jan said. 'We married too young. Do you think there should be two marriages for everyone, one for when we are young, and one for when we mature?'

'But what if one matures away from the other?' That might apply to John and Jan. 'Do you believe that happens?'

'In my case, yes. But my rival is not a man but my granddaughter.' He laughed. 'Bella is besotted with Rosabel, and her bringing up.'

'Have you spoken to her about it?'

'No, but I have to Rose's husband. We laugh about it. He has said, "As long as Bella doesn't get into bed with us, it's all right by me." '

'Perhaps the Krasnapolsky was to blame.' She made the remark idly, thinking, I bet he's wrong, and his rival is a man. At the same time, she was wishing he would slow down a bit. The road twisted and turned, John had always anticipated bends, because she suffered from travel sickness. She knew Jan Graf glanced at her.

'But you're not far wrong,' he said. 'Bella was an only child, and she loved going to the Krasnapolsky, perhaps she believed it was a microcosm of family life. She would have liked more children.'

'We were quite happy with one. Perhaps you should find a rival for Rosabel.' She was appalled at what she had just said. She wasn't thinking straight. She wished he would slow down.

'*Bonne idée*,' he said, laughing.

When they got back to Laborie and her cottage, wishing to eradicate her comment, she said, 'Can I offer you a drink?' thinking it would sound neighbourly and sophisticated.

She felt him looking at her, his hands still on the wheel, and she thought, Wrong again. I'm not really good at being sophisticated, or is it that I'm still regretting Roger?

'I'd like that,' he said. 'At least there are no neighbours here to talk about us.'

They sat in the kitchen at first, where she kept the

drinks, but feeling uneasy, she said, 'Let's sit in the *bolet* and see the view. You won't have one being in a hollow. I love my view.'

'OK,' he said. 'Let me take that tray.' She thought his look was quizzical, as if he was trying to solve a puzzle. Is he thinking I'm being a tease? she wondered, sitting with him and watching the car lights drawing a circle round the castle at Gramon in the distance.

Strangely enough, her mind was full of Roger Mills. It was typical of Dr Moir that he hadn't told her he had engaged a temporary assistant, taking it for granted that she would give Roger bed and board. Her irritation with Dr Moir for assuming that she would act as housekeeper was soon dispelled. She could not possibly feel any ill-will towards such a charming young man who helped to clear the table, fill the coal bucket and play with Scott, who in his turn showed his appreciation by calling him 'Daddy'.

This, of course, broke the ice. She couldn't possibly stand on her dignity, and they became friends almost instantly, and to her he was like a substitute for John. He praised her cooking, and her dresses, joked with her, played records for her in the evening.

Once, when he put on one of Jean Sablon's, a favourite of hers at the time, his eyes had beckoned hers across the room and he got to his feet and held out his arms to her. She had stood up too, and gone into them. She couldn't say he reminded her then of John, who had never been a dancer, and had brown eyes not grey like this man's, which met hers and smiled down on her as they danced. When she had said she must get to bed, he had nodded and steered her into the corridor still in his arms, pausing at her bedroom door, his eyes still on her. Laughingly she had said, 'I'd like to ask you in for coffee,' and he had said, 'It's not coffee I want.'

All kinds of ideas had run through her head when she was in bed: had she heard him aright, and if she had, that the idea was impossible, John was in the war fighting for her, Scott was sleeping at her side in his cot, but, she thought now, sitting beside Jan Graf, if she had known what she had found out later, things might have been different. Because she had wanted Roger that night.

Now, she thought, here was yet another chance to level the score. What are you thinking of? she asked herself. John is dead. Besides, Jan Graf hasn't the appeal Roger Mills had, but she had been younger then, and so had Roger.

Everything she said to Jan Graf seemed loaded. Was it that she had the capacity for making misleading remarks to men through lack of experience, or was she now a better judge of her own behaviour? Be that as it may, there was no romance here, it would be a cold coupling.

Later, when Jan was talking about Bella, she said, 'Her obsession with the baby, if that's what it is, will pass.' It was a remark made to fill a gap, a stupid remark she thought. 'You should try to occupy your mind with someone else.' The words fell into the silence, like the heavy clanging of a bell. Oh, stupid, stupid, she thought.

'That's what I'm doing,' he said, and getting up, pulled her to her feet and kissed her hard on the mouth.

'You shouldn't have done that,' she said.

'Why?'

'Are you going?' she said, ignoring the question.

'Not unless you ask me to stay.'

'I'm not likely to do that. People might talk.'

'Which people?'

'Oh, country people. They are like animals. Their ears and eyes are better than ours.' Now she *was* talking nonsense.

'We don't count them. Boris and Hazel are away.'

She laughed. 'I have only your word for that.'

'I gather you don't want me to stay?'

'I don't want you to stay.' It had to be said.

He waved when he was in the car, not looking too downcast, and sounded the horn as he turned the corner. Two down, she thought. Chances will come less often now.

She went about her household tasks the following morning, but feeling she couldn't live with herself, she decided to have a walk. Walking had always been her cure for feeling bad about herself, but she needed an object, be it only posting a letter. She daren't walk down the hill in case she met Jan or perhaps the Halliwells, so she set off with a basket with the intention of going through the wood at the back of her cottage in search of mushrooms. Agnès, of the farm, had once taught her how to recognize the various varieties: *morelles*, *girolles*, *cêpes*, *chantelles*, were the ones most likely to be found here. The concentration required, the undiluted joy when she found a clump of *cêpes*, and the pleasure of identification, took her mind away from any worries. The feeling of being at one with Nature, and finding something which was a bounty, a gift, was enough to place these worries in proper perspective. She made up her mind that she would share this bounty with Hazel and Boris. They would make a Welcome Home gift. Jan had said they were due this morning. If she were lucky she wouldn't see him.

She enjoyed the gloom in the wood, the rustling noises

around her of birds. Once she and John had disturbed a *sanglier*, and it had made off, followed by a family of little piglets, in a line behind it. The day suited her mood, her doubts about herself. Had she been leading Jan on, or had he thought she was? The trouble was that in one's fifties, one couldn't flirt like a young girl, and innocent remarks seemed to take on a double meaning. The trouble is, she told herself, you're not at ease with yourself, or your age.

When she emerged from the top of the wood at a well-remembered cherry tree, which they used to raid, she saw Benoit working amongst his tobacco plants. '*Bonjour, Benoit*,' she said: '*Regardez!*' She held out her basket to him for inspection. '*Qu'en pensez vous?*'

He turned over her crop with a stubby forefinger. '*Bon! Mais, soyez sage! Qui est votre professeur?*'

'*Votre fille.*'

'*Ah! Maintenant elle est occupée avec la petite, pas de champignons.*'

'*C'est ça.*'

She walked on after chattng for a little while. She was making a circular detour behind the hamlet, and when she came near the Halliwell's caravan, she saw Hazel and waved.

'Hello,' she called. 'I've brought you a present. I heard you had gone to Toulouse.'

'Yes, we had a good time. Boris has driven to Gramon to arrange for some help with the roof. He assures me the house will be finished in a week or two.'

'That's good news. So you've had a change of heart? I'm glad. I could do with your company.'

'Jan Graf set off for Amsterdam this morning. He's hoping to come back with his wife.'

'Oh, is he?' She felt Hazel's eyes on her.

'Have you been seeing him?'

'He took me out to dinner last night. He didn't say anything to me about going back to Amsterdam, but then, why should he?'

'You know the answer to that. Come into the caravan and have a coffee.'

'Thanks. That would be lovely.'

'Are you having one of your days?'

'No, I've been walking all morning. Days?'

'Have you forgotten? You once confided to me that you missed John here more than you did at home.'

'Perhaps because we were happiest here. Neither of us liked where we lived in England. We always intended to get out of it, and then he died . . .'

'Yes, that was tough for you. Come in, then. I'll change that offer of coffee to plum brandy made by Benoit in his illicit still.'

'He gave *you* some? Me too. Hush money.'

'I don't mind being hushed. So you had dinner with Jan Graf?'

'Yes. He's worried about Bella's obsession with their little granddaughter, he says.'

'Well, that's a change. In his shoes, I would have worried about another man. She's a charmer. Have another brandy and tell me more.'

'I've a feeling he was pulling my leg.' Were his remarks about the little granddaughter just that? I'll never be sophisticated, she thought. 'Yes, thank you, Hazel,' she said, 'just a spot.'

Nine

S itting in the garden the following morning, Jane turned over in her mind the outing with Jan Graf. Why had it made her feel uneasy? There was his driving, of course, and also when he had pulled her to her feet, when they were sitting in the *bolet*, and kissed her.

Her mind had gone back then to Roger Mills, and how he had attracted her. Was she only discovering her sexuality now when it was too late? At fifty-four? After the honeymoon period with John, hadn't she been too preoccupied with Scott and the practice to remain his lover? And when he was away, wasn't her captivation with Roger Mills a sign of her longing for John? And now, she thought, you're worried because you feel you led Jan Graf on last night. You're not a woman of the world. You're uneasy because you're dissatisfied with your behaviour. Had she drunk too much? She knew champagne always made her heady.

And apropos his driving, who are you to criticize? she asked herself. You've never been a driver. The reason you gave yourself was that they had only one car in the practice, and she and John had never had enough money to buy another one.

There was that time when she had offered to deliver medicine to one of John's patients.

She had liked to imagine herself as competent, after all she had been a businesswoman before she married, and when John had said to her between afternoon and evening surgery, 'I'm worried. A young woman came to see me this afternoon with a sick baby. Esther wasn't there to make up the prescription for her. I said I would arrange to have it handed in. Why I said that I don't know, except that I was sorry for her. Her husband was killed in the Middle East three months ago. The surgery will go on and on. Moir isn't coming in.'

'Let me do it,' she said. 'Scott's asleep. You could run up occasionally and see that he's all right. Tell me the address.'

'It's too far to walk,' he said, 'it's one of those streets running down to the river.'

'I'll drive.'

'Are you sure?' he said.

'Sure I'm sure.'

He had made up the prescription and given her the bottle and the address, and she had set off, first making sure Scott was all right. He looked happily asleep in his cot, and she thought how lucky she was compared with this poor woman without a husband, and with a sick baby.

She felt competent, and drove to where she thought she would find the house, but she had been wrong. The street she was in was a dead end, and there was no room to turn, so she decided to back up its length. Halfway along she felt a bump, and stopped immediately, her heart in her mouth. All her confidence had left her. In trepidation she got out of the car.

A woman was kneeling on the road beside a little girl who seemed to be unconscious. She looked up accusingly at Jane. 'You backed into her,' she wailed.

91

Jane was trembling. 'Oh, no, I was looking in my mirror all the time. I didn't see anyone.' She knelt down beside the woman. 'I'm Dr Maxwell's wife. I was delivering medicine near here.'

The woman ignored what Jane was saying. 'She's not breathing! Maybe she's . . . I'll have to get her to the hospital!'

Jane closed her eyes in terror. 'No, I'm sure she's all right. She's just been stunned. But I assure you there was no one on the road when I was backing.'

A man was standing beside them. 'I saw your lass run out from behind your house, missus,' he said. 'She was following a ball.'

Jane looked around. There was a ball lying in the gutter which bore out his story. Now there was a group of women standing on the pavement, talking together. They looked accusingly at her. She said to the man, 'Will you help me to lift her, and I'll take her to the hospital?'

'I'm coming too,' the woman said. She was crying. The women had drawn near, and were eyeing Jane coldly. 'Aye, on you go, Jean,' one of them said.

Jane helped the mother into the back seat where they had put the little girl who was now stirring, much to Jane's relief. She was still in a state of terror exacerbated by lifting the girl and having seen blood on her forehead. What would John say? And there was the woman who was waiting for the medicine . . .

She said to the man who was still there. 'I was on my way to Mrs Lawson at 53, South Terrace.'

One of the women said, 'That's the woman who lost her man.'

'That's right,' Jane said. Then to the man who was

standing at the kerb: 'Do you think you could hand in the medicine to Mrs Lawson? Is it near?'

'Aye, the next turning. I'll do that.' She reached into the front seat for the bottle.

'Don't worry,' she spoke to the woman in the back.

'She's moving! We better get on.'

'Yes. Right.' She handed the man the bottle, got into the front seat, and drove away carefully. Her arms felt useless, but she gripped the wheel to steady herself, keeping her eyes on the road. This can't have happened, she thought, but it was reality, the mean street, the little group in her mirror, talking, the woman behind her with her daughter, who was now conscious. 'Where are we going, Ma?' Jane heard her say. She was tormented by the thought that she should have asked the man if there was a telephone box near, so that she could have phoned for an ambulance. But, no, this would be quicker, and the little girl seemed to be recovering, at least she was now crying weakly, and her mother was saying 'Shh, shh!' Jane, listening to her comforting words, couldn't believe she had got herself into this situation. But surely the girl hadn't been there when she was backing? Wasn't it more likely that she had run out after the ball when Jane had taken her eyes off the mirror for a second? 'We'll soon be at the hospital,' she said, 'Try not to worry.' There was no reply from the back.

Now she had a new worry which was tormenting her. She should have phoned John, or maybe driven back to the surgery with the girl. She was still doubtful when she reached the hospital, where she parked and got out, opened the back door and with the help of the woman, managed to get the girl in her arms. Her mother followed behind, asking questions. She felt totally unable to reassure her. What if the girl was badly injured, or worse, died? She could see the evening paper: 'Doctor's wife in serious accident involving girl of seven'. You're totally unprepared to cope with this situation, she told herself, because of the quiet life you lead. You shouldn't have been so eager to step out of your role.

She sat beside the girl's mother while she answered the questions the nurse asked her. When the nurse looked at her, she said, 'I'm Dr Maxwell's wife,' and saw her head go up. She stayed with the mother, Mrs Thompson (she had noted her name while the nurse was questioning her), while her daughter was wheeled away to be examined.

A doctor appeared quite soon and looking at Jane said, 'There's no need for you to wait, Mrs Maxwell. The police will call to get particulars from you . . .' And then to Mrs Thompson: 'Your little girl's going to be all right,' and seeing Jane had got to her feet said, it seemed with emphasis, 'Drive carefully.' She took it as a reprimand.

She drove back slowly, and when she had parked the car, she went straight upstairs and found Scott lying awake in his cot, waving his arms. She lifted him and held him closely. 'Oh, Scott,' she said, 'I've been such a fool!' She had never in her life wept such bitter tears.

She was sitting on their bed, cradling the baby when John came bursting in. 'You're back soon. Did you find the place?'

'Yes, oh, John, I've done a terrible thing.' She recounted the accident to him, and saw his smile disappear. He was silent for a moment.

'Did you get the name of this man as witness?'

'No. But he knew the girl's mother. Perhaps if you could call at her house, she would give you his address.'

'I'll do that right away.'

'What if the police come while you're gone?'

'I shan't be long. Don't worry. It's the practice car. I'll have to tell Dr Moir.'

She wept while she was tucking the baby into his cot, and while she got the supper ready. So much for your attempt to step out of your role, she thought. I'll never drive again.

Thinking of the occurrence now, in Laborie, she relived the incident. A further indication of her lack of worldliness, or her lack of confidence in herself, she thought, which she had felt yesterday with Jan Graf.

And with Roger Mills also. She had been attracted by his whole persona, his Southern Counties voice, his sweetness, his tales of his family in Hampshire, by his total difference from John, making him seem homespun, and in an effort to hide this attraction she had probaby given the impression of an unschooled girl instead of a married woman.

She thought in pictures. She saw him coming into the sitting room after surgery, collapsing on to that brown sofa, and saying, 'You have to watch old so-and-so downstairs and the plump maiden. I think there's a *thing* going on there!' And to Scott, who was pulling at his arm, 'OK old chap, I'll be with you in a second.' And then there was the evening when they danced. The feel of his body. Broader than John's, different smell.

She remembered how he had consoled her during the agony of waiting for the case to come up (John had been on leave when the accident occurred but was now back with his regiment). Roger had made light of it. 'My younger sister has had several accidents with her car. She has a sports job and drives like the wind. Dad has threatened to take it away from her. He spoils her.'

95

Dr Moir had not given her any support. He had pursed his lips when she had apologized to him, but hadn't offered any comfort to her. She had felt she had prejudiced him against John by her carelessness.

She and John had discussed his situation in the practice many times, and had decided that a bird in hand was worth two in the bush. It might be difficult to find a job when he came out of the Army. Better to have a jumping-off place. After all, Dr Moir had not reneged on his agreement.

On the evening of the day when John had left, she had felt utterly stranded. She hated the place, hated Dr Moir. Roger's arrival shortly afterwards brought light to her life. Scott regarded him as a substitute. To her he was different but delightful. He was a man in the house.

She looked up from her lofty seat on the *bolet* to see Boris coming across the grass to her. He waved, and came up the steps, sinking down on a seat beside her. 'That hill gets me down. I'm getting old.'

'Why didn't you drive?'

'Exercise. I came to add my thanks for the mushrooms. They were delightful. Do you know what *girolles* cost in London just now? No wonder the restaurants are able to charge such prices.'

'Well, all fungi cost here is an early start and a keen eye. Good for walking off the black dog, as Churchill called it.'

'I never think of you like that. You have a most serene exterior.'

'That's my cover-up. Don't you ever have regrets, Boris?'

'Plenty. But I don't dwell on them. Business life trains you out of that.'

'Pity I didn't have that training. I had to give up a job in the business world when I got married. It was the rule then. I missed it. If you have a mind at all you sometimes think you're losing it when you become a housewife and mother. I once had an accident when I was driving someone else's car. I wanted to prove to myself that I could operate away from the kitchen sink.'

'How long ago was that?'

'About thirty years ago.'

'And it still rankles?'

'Yes.'

'Nothing more recent than that?'

She thought of her outing with Jan Graf. 'Not directly.'

'I'll make a guess. It's when you step out of character that you have regrets.'

'You're right.'

'I came up to see if you would like to go to the Mechoui with Hazel and I next month. She's got to know quite a few people at St. Martin, and says it should be great fun.'

'That's good of you. I should be very pleased to go. Take me out of myself, as they say.'

'I'm going to St. Martin this morning to buy the tickets. You might like to come if you have any shopping to do.'

'Thank you. Sit there and I'll go in and get my shopping bag.'

Driving along the twisting road to St. Martin she noticed how careful Boris was. 'Hazel was telling me you've lost your neighbours?' she mentioned, casually she hoped.

'Yes. We think there's trouble with the marriage. His wife and daughter went off with the baby, and he seemed to be very disappointed that he wasn't allowed to drive them.'

'I wonder why?'

'Could be that they don't like his driving. Hazel accepted a lift to Gramon from him one morning, and she said it was a hair-raising experience.'

She decided to confide in him. 'While you and Hazel were in Toulouse, he took me out to dinner. I know what Hazel means.'

'How did that go?'

'Oh, all right. We went to the Pont l'Isle. It's become the place to go to since I was last there with John.'

'Busy?'

'Yes. The food's good.'

'Well, I won't be outdone by Jan Graf. I'll take you and Hazel on an evening to be arranged. I like to copy their dishes, if possible.'

'You're very good to me, you and Hazel.'

'We're very fond of you, and we like to keep an eye on you.'

They drove into the middle of St. Martin and Boris parked his car at the town hall, a one-storied building recognizable by the plethora of notices stuck on the wooden door. They both went to read them. 'Missing. Mademoiselle Grelier's cat, Mimi. Should anyone find it, please bring it back. She is devastated.' 'Meeting of the War Graves Commission, 3rd August, 1971 at Town Hall, Gramon.' Then a notice, ringed in red: 'Please apply for tickets at Town Hall for Mechoui, 31st July,

1971. Dancing to Remy Boys from 10.00 p.m.' 'Youth Club on Wednesday as usual.'

'Does that date suit you?' Boris asked. He had his finger on the notice.

'Yes, fine. I'm going to visit Valerie and Scott the week before. I'll make a point of being back in time.'

'Supposing we go to the Pont l'Isle before the Mechoui.'

'And miss the eats?'

'Well, perhaps that isn't a good idea. We'll let Hazel be the arbiter.'

When Boris was driving her home he asked her, 'Have you any regrets about coming here to live?'

'None. Of course, I'll have to see what it's like to be here in winter. Have you?'

'None, but then I've had the house to occupy myself with. But I've grown to like the pace of life here. Hazel finds it difficult to adapt.'

'She has to have her alternatives. You're lucky, of course, being able to keep on your London house.'

'Yes. You're different from Hazel. You have re-sources. I think if Hazel would give herself longer here, she would find some too.'

'I'm sure she would. I think she would find some kindred spirits in Gramon. And it would be lovely for me, having her here.'

'Remember when we first met at St. Martin?'

'Of couse I do. We were so pleased to find you two. Our French was non-existent. And then Raoul and Margo joined us, remember? They were staying in the hotel at the time while their house was being renovated.'

'Yes. John admired Margo, I think.'

'You know he did. Didn't you?' She smiled.

'Of course I did. Any man would.'

Any man would, she thought. Supremely confident Margo. The type of woman who made all married women feaful.

When she was making her supper after Boris had dropped her off, her mind turned to her first introduction to the south-west of France and St. Martin. What good times those had been! The dining together, the talk, she usually more silent than Hazel and Margo, but always finding support from Boris. John was a ladies' man, she had discovered. There was no socializing at Tynebay, even when he had come back from the Army. He had been too busy, and they had got into the habit of spending time together alone in the evenings, assuring each other that they liked it that way.

One evening in Tynebay, over dinner, he had said, 'I have two weeks' holiday coming up. Do you want to go back to Scotland? To your aunt and uncle's in Fifeshire?'

'No.' The year was 1951, Scott was eight years of age. 'What about Scott?'

'We'd take him. Remember I told you about that place called Gramon in France where I worked as a waiter during one vacation?'

'Yes.'

'It's lovely country. Perigord. What do you say if we take the train to the south coast, then cross by ferry to Le Havre? Scott can sleep on the boat, so can we, then when we get to France, hiring a car and driving down through the west side to the Limousin. We're practically at Perigord when we reach Brive. I can remember the journey well, I did it with a university friend in his clapped-out Mini, and we hit on this hotel in Gramon, where we were so skinned that we asked if they could give us any work. Washing up and peeling potatoes, that's about all I remember, but on our days off we toured the region, and I still remember it: castles, rivers, huddled villages of stone-built cottages, it's a lovely honey-coloured stone, kindly people, gorgeous weather, wild flowers, hidden lanes, pubs . . .'

'You make it sound like paradise.'

'Sunshine, bathing in the river Lot, you'd love it, so would Scott. There are caves to be seen. He'd love that.'

'Could we afford it?' She had a flash of memory of the three of them in a cave on all fours following the guide, who every time he turned his head to speak to them, gave them a blast from his garlic-laden breath. They had laughed and held their noses, unbeknown to him.

'We don't spend money here, and the only expense would be getting there . . . Let's do it, Jane, we owe it to ourselves.'

The contrast between this strange region called Perigord and here, she thought, yes, we owe it to ourselves.

It was on the way through France that they began to talk about buying a house, a cottage, a retreat, according to John they were for sale for nothing at all. He had been left a few thousands in his father's will. And when they arrived at Gramon on market day she fell in love with it, the perfect market town with its castle and river, and even more so, the surrounding countryside. The next day they were installed at the small hotel in St. Martin. It was to be their base while they looked around.

Boris and Hazel were staying there too, and on the same quest as they were, although in their case, it was land they were after. Boris intended to build a house. He had got to know the region when he had deviated from the N20 on his way to Spain, and it had exercised its charm on him too. Hazel was dubious.

101

And the bonus had been Raoul and Margo Traigo, who were staying in the hotel. Raoul was Spanish, Margo came from London, and they had met in Valencia, when she had been touring Spain with her former husband.

What good times they had had together, three couples, aged between thirty and forty, pioneers in the French countryside, adventurous, eager to leave city life behind them and find the Good Life in a foreign country.

She thought of the evening when the Halliwells and they had been invited to dinner at Raoul and Margo's house, a huge stone edifice, with a well in the garden, badly neglected. The staircase had collapsed, and the bedrooms were reached by a step-ladder.

Raoul was the cook, and he had prepared a selection of tapas, which were so varied that they hardly needed to eat the paellas he had also made. The Traigos had acquired a huge table which only partially filled the room, and the food was arranged on it, with bottles of wine at strategic intervals. They were encouraged to help themselves. It made for a relaxed atmosphere, backed by Spanish flamenco records which Raoul played. Everyone was happy. The windows were open and the night noises came to them: the ripple of a stream which ran through the garden; birds settling in the trees and making a fuss about it; and the occasional hoot of an owl.

Margo got up and was dancing on her own, drifting about the room in time to the music. She beckoned to John. 'Come on, Johnnie, surely you can dance.'

'I'm the world's worst,' he said, laughing. 'Ask Jane.'

'Then I'll teach you.' She was charming, flashing white smile, face flushed, black hair loose, incredibly slender ankles beneath her black skirt.

102

'Go on, John!' Boris shouted. 'Have a bash!'

John got up, and with one arm raised in the air, circled Margo, adopting a peculiar, clicking step, which reduced the rest of them to helpless laughter. He was a clown, Jane thought, swerving, bowing, circling, then taking Margo in his arms and swirling her round and round.

Raoul shouted, 'Bravo, John! Try the tango now.'

'You want the tango? I give you the tango!' He was having one of his 'daft fits', as Jane called it. He sometimes romped with Scott, making him giggle with his antics. He seized Margo round the waist, and with their arms outstretched in front of them, they charged round the room. Raoul began to clap in time to the music, and the other three joined in.

'Oh, John!' Jane said, admiring him for being able to make a fool of himself. She could never do it.

Boris' eyes met her in amusement, and he got to his feet. 'Come on, Jane, we'll show them!' He grasped her round the waist, and they also charged round the room, laughing, colliding with Margo and John, Hazel and Raoul joined them, and the three couples danced until they tired themselves out. John was the chief performer, Jane noticed, as he swung Margo round, bent her over his arm, and clicked his heels like a flamenco dancer, shouting '*Olé!*' from time to time. She saw Raoul and Boris laughing in appreciation, possibly envy. There had been no chance in Tynebay for him to display this side of his character. No parties. Whose fault was that? But certainly no encouragement from her.

What good times we had then, she thought, remembering how, when exhausted, they had all flung themselves down on chairs, while Raoul plied them with food and wine. John had been able to let himself go, she thought. Was I too staid for him? That night, she remembered, he and Margo had strolled in the garden, while she sat and talked with Raoul. 'Your John is a comedian,' he had said to her.

She had thought, This is a side of John I rarely see. He's like a boy let out of school. He came home from the Army, looking young, handsome and full of life, but over the years in that miserable practice, gradually he lost his sense of fun. Whose fault was it? Was it mine?

But when they were at Laborie, they seemed to come together again. It had had a good effect on her, the cloud hanging over her which was the remembrance of her mother's suicide, disappeared.

But Raoul and Margo had dropped out of their lives. 'They sold the house,' Hazel and Boris had told them, when they went back the next summer, 'and we think they split up. She met someone else . . .'

It might have been John, she thought. I was lucky he didn't fall for her. Or did he? Had he been tempted, and had his love for her won over temptation? Was the truth of the matter that he was easily attracted to women, always had been, and she had not been exciting enough for him?

She remembered that evening when Raoul had driven over, visibly upset because Margo wouldn't come downstairs for dinner. They had been quarrelling, could John help? Looking at Raoul, she had seen his Spanishness, and thought that he and Margo weren't a good combination.

John had looked doubtful. Raoul and Boris always paid homage to the fact that he was a special kind of doctor, because he had once said he had experience in a mental hospital, and they assumed therefore that he had extra insight into the mind. 'All right,' he said. 'I'll see what I can do,' and went to get his case.

'You come too, Jane,' Raoul said. 'She might be glad to see you.'

They drove to that large house of the Traigos, for which he had so many plans. They still hadn't had the circular staircase installed, the step-ladder was still in place, the huge dark room which had to have French windows was still dark, with windows which didn't let one see the beautiful view of the garden and the landscape beyond, and the floor of the hall was still being laid with flagstones by Raoul, and one had to walk on wooden planks. His plans had been numerous, but hadn't come to fruition yet.

They stood in the dark hall, and upstairs they could hear the mournful sound of Margo weeping.

John shouted, his voice echoing round the hall, 'I'm coming up to see if I can help, Margo,' and was rewarded by a outburst of weeping and screaming. She sounds like a naughty child, Jane thought, and looked at John, who was already climbing the ladder, his case in his hand. 'It's all right,' he was shouting.

Raoul said, 'Come and we'll walk in the garden, Jane,' and there he had embarrassed her by telling her how much he loved Margo, and how he couldn't possibly live without her. 'She's always been difficult,' he said, 'but then, she's so highly-strung. I lose my temper with her sometimes.'

She thought, What does he mean? At a loss, she put her arm round his shoulders, and said, 'Don't worry. John's marvellous with people. He'll quieten her down,' at the same time wondering how she had formed that opinion, as he hadn't had any such experience with her.

Her temper was too much under control. Raoul put his arm round her waist and squeezed it, and said she was wonderful, they all thought that, they were a wonderful couple. And, after walking for some time, while he continued to tell her about his life with Margo, they went back into the house.

The huge hall was in darkness, and she thought, It's so quiet, what are they doing up there? Raoul led her into the large room which was darker than ever now, and poured out two glasses of cognac, saying, 'We need this.'

She sat in miserable silence, at least it was miserable to her, while Raoul continued to unburden himself, and told her how he and Margo had met in Valencia, and fallen madly in love. She had come there with her husband, and they had put up at Raoul's hotel. 'What a woman!' he said appreciatively.

She had felt that this was a situation she certainly couldn't deal with, but luckily Margo appeared with John, and they were both smiling, and then the four of them were laughing as if nothing had happened. 'That step-ladder, Raoul,' John said. 'I nearly broke my neck on it. Anyhow, she's all right now. Aren't you, Margo?'

'I have upset you, my darling,' Raoul said to her. 'Come and sit down and have a cognac.' Jane wondered if the cognac hadn't been the cause of the upset.

She noticed Margo was flushed and her hand was shaking as she held the glass. She raised it to Jane and said, 'You're lucky to have a husband like John, Jane.'

What did one say to that, she wondered, but looking at him and raising her glass, jokingly, she thought he looked like Scott when he was naughty.

He had told her later in the car that Margo had been hysterical, and that he thought she and Raoul hit the

106

bottle. He had talked to her, or rather listened to her, and given her a sedative to take later, which would calm her down for the rest of the night.

'I wouldn't be surprised if they go in for a lot of drinking,' she said, and he said that he had gathered Raoul ill-treated her, but how could you believe her? The lives some people lived would surprise you.

'Do you believe he may physically maltreat her?' she asked him, and he said he would believe anything of them.

It seemed too petty and childish to say that the whole business had upset her, and she would be glad if the Traigos moved away. But for a long time she couldn't stop thinking of standing in that dark hall and listening to the silence above.

Ten

1971

It was Sunday morning, and Valerie and Scott were sitting in the garden of their house in Notting Hill. The garden had been the deciding factor in buying the house. It was a long oblong and, being at the end of the road, was enclosed by a stone wall against which grew some old trees, mostly fruit, with gnarled branches. In the centre of the lawn was a mulberry tree surrounded by flagging on which their deckchairs had been placed. The previous owner had told them that the houses in the road were built on the estate of an old mansion, and the trees had belonged to it. The bushes in the borders gave a rather gloomy effect, mostly holly, but Valerie had the intention of putting colourful perennials in between them.

'I think Mother would like it here,' Scott said, 'and the basement flat could be made nice for her when some of her furniture is taken out of store. And she would have her own entrance from the front. I've written to her.'

'Do you think she would like being with us? She's a very private lady.'

'Darling, you're not listening. She would have her own entrance. She could come and go as she pleased.'

'Has she any friends in London?'

'Not that I know of. But she would have us, and the garden, and there are museums and the theatre. She's very resourceful. Although she wouldn't be in London very much, I like to think the flat would be here for her when she felt like it. I worry about her on her own.'

'But it's her choice.'

'Yes, I know. But there's a strong bond between us. I realized it when Father died, as if I had to step into his place.'

'And then I came along. But I don't think she ever resented me.'

'Never. She admires you and the life you lead. She feels she has nothing to offer. I'm sure that's what's behind her writing. She would like to have had a career, but then there was the war, and me, and the practice. She felt obliged to the senior partner to run it, and I think Dr Moir expected it of her. It was a kind of quid pro quo arrangement, but he treated her as an employee and she seemed to accept that. She had a great respect for authority. Her sense of duty was tremendous. When I was young there were strict rules: I mustn't play on the stairs or make a noise when the surgeries were on, or go down to the dispensary. Esther, the dispenser, used to let me wash the bottles which I loved to do, and she would allow me to hand out the medicine to the patients through the window opening.'

'So that was the beginning of your wish to be a doctor?'

'Partly. I loved the smells. But it was chiefly that I admired my father, and it pleased him immensely when I went to Durham. When he died, I was there, and she must have been pretty lonely in that great gaunt house which she hated. She used to apologize to the domestics who had to clean it. Once, when one of them hadn't turned up, I caught her scrubbing the floor of the waiting room. "It's got to be done," she said, when I remonstrated with her. I think she had always promised herself that she would go to Laborie when I graduated. That had been their plan.'

'I expect it gave her immense satisfaction to leave Dr Moir.'

'Oh, she didn't leave him in the lurch. Her sense of duty was too strong. But he had to employ a housekeeper in her place. She once said to me, "That will show him what I was worth." Her salary was permission to live in the house. It was a roof over her head, and for him a cheap way of running the practice. During the war when my father was away, she had to provide bed and board for temporary doctors. I remember one, a young man, who played with me. I thought he was my daddy. When there was an air-raid warning, the three of us went downstairs to the Morrison shelter.'

'Did your father leave much?'

'Enough for Mother, fortunately, to go and live in France. Dr Moir was pretty mean. Looking back, I can't understand why they didn't move away from Tynebay since they both hated it so much.'

'Perhaps they were too tired to make a move.'

'Yes, that could be it. According to Mother, they had great times together before they went there. She was convinced that the job killed him. There was a great turnout at his funeral. Greatly loved, they said.' His voice broke.

'Don't distress yourself, darling.' Valerie got up and stood behind him, her hands on his shoulders, and kissed the top of his head. He reached up and took one of her

110

hands. 'It's a sad story,' she said. 'However, she'll be glad to see you getting on.'

'Yes. That's why I'd like to give her a home here when she wants it. She'd never ask. You know I never saw much in Laborie. She's living on her memories there, happy ones. They adored it, the freedom and the countryside. I guess I'm an urban type.'

'I'm feeling quite sad. Why don't you go in and bring us some wine?'

'OK.'

'I'll look forward to getting to know your mother better when she comes here. Perhaps we can do things together. She always strikes me as rather shy, she's like a child, somehow, as if she hasn't grown up enough to handle grown-up situations. Sometimes we laugh together as if we were girls of the same age, other times she shuts herself off.'

'I'll get that wine.'

I'll go the last week in June, Jane thought, folding Scott's letter. Then I'll be back in time for the Mechoui. It's good of them to offer me the basement flat at their house. And Scott is arranging with that repository in Tynebay to send our own furniture down. There wasn't much as the place was furnished when we moved in. What a relief it was to see the last of that brown velvet three-piece! But, oh, the joy when we saw the huge bed in the bedroom! But that tube! The bane of John's existence. Stella Moir felt the same about it . . . Did I miss out on the chance to help her? I had never come across anyone like her, and I was too young to understand.

I wonder how I'll get on with Valerie. I want her to love me, not to get in the way of Scott and her. To be so clever and so young. She did better in exams than he did. Neither he nor John shone at exams. It would be nice if she and I could go to a matinée together, if she weren't on duty. I suppose we couldn't shop together either. But of course, I shall have to make it quite clear to them that there's no need to include me in their dinner at night, but perhaps they would allow me to cook it for them. They must be weary when they come home. Remember how John used to come bounding upstairs after the surgeries and say, 'Thank God that's over!' He was a dogsbody to that man for years, because he refused to take on another partner. He didn't like me. That was evident after that accident with his car. And did he resent me going out with Stella in *her* car? Or did they both resent us because we had Scott? An odd couple. I often wondered if Esther had told him that his wife had called for me in her car, and perhaps he had reproached Stella for buying it. Perhaps he had thought she wasn't safe. But it was a sad end for her . . .

If Jan Graf comes back to Laborie with or without his wife, it will be good for him to see that I'm not at home pining for his return. Strange, his dashing off the following morning after taking me out to dinner. Difficult to understand.

To have two homes will be nice. I've always wanted to explore London, see the sights, live a cosmopolitan life. Yet I'm too fond of this place. It's near nature, and John . . .

Eleven

The taxi man was there, holding his board to his chest, 'MRS. MAXWELL'. Neither Scott nor Valerie could meet her as they would both be busy, and this was the arrangement they had made. Driving through London, she thought it seemed more crowded and dirtier than she remembered. She sat beside the driver, and they chatted most of the way, he telling her about his family, and she making the remarks required of her, which she had always found easy to do.

He agreed with her about the noisiness and dirtiness of London, but said it depended on which part you were in. Where her son lived was very nice and quiet, genteel. When he stopped at what seemed a tall, forbidding-looking house, he said, 'Well, here you are,' and offered to carry her case to the door.

Following Scott's instructions, she directed him to the basement flat, thanked him and said, 'How much was that?' but he said Dr Maxwell had 'seen to it'. However, as he seemed to be looking expectantly at her, she gave him one of the five-pound notes she had ready. He seemed pleased with this, and went off with a cheerful 'Good luck, Mrs Maxwell.'

Scott must have said she was his mother. It made her feel at home, and she extracted the keys from behind a

113

loose brick he had told her about, opened the door and went into the flat.

It had been furnished with some of the pieces from the repository, and instantly it brought back John to her. She hadn't thought it worthwhile transporting what furniture they had to Laborie, which they had furnished some time ago locally. Now she saw a chair which she had been fond of, a nursing chair which she had used for Scott, which with its long back was particularly comfortable. And there was a desk chair which she could do with when she was writing at the table in Laborie. But the point was that between them Valerie and Scott had furnished the place for her very adequately, and now she saw the flowers, lilies, on the table, with a note propped in front of them: 'Make yourself a cup of tea. Everything you need is in the kitchen. We'll be home by seven o'clock, at least one of us will.' Strong handwriting, she thought. She was lucky to have such a good daughter-in-law.

Actually it was Scott who was in first. He came down the inside stairs in a rush, and found her sitting on the nursing chair. 'Mother, how good to see you!' he said. He came forward to greet her, and she got up from the chair to meet him. 'Have you been waiting long?'

'No, only about half an hour. I made myself a cup of tea as Valerie said. How are you, Scott? Are you terribly busy?'

'Not too bad. Come upstairs, and we'll have a drink and wait for Valerie. I'm taking you out to dinner to-night.'

'That will be lovely. But I intend to cook for you when you come home, you and Valerie, if you'll let me.'

'We'll talk about that later. Oh, hello, darling.' He turned as Valerie came into the room, went towards her and they kissed. She was glad to see that he copied his father in that.

'Well, Jane, you got here. Good journey?' Valerie came to where she was sitting, bent forward and kissed her on the cheek. 'I'm sorry I wasn't there to welcome you, but I got held up.'

'What was it?' Scott asked.

'Child of five presenting with sickness and diarrhoea. Persistent temperature. We eliminated all the possibilities then . . . I'll tell you later.' Jane could imagine them discussing the case in bed, and he perhaps telling her about his day. She had always listened to John, if he was worried, and wanted to talk, but generally he kept his worries to himself, because she wouldn't have been able to understand, she thought now. How lucky Scott was to have a wife who could listen with understanding. When she thought now of all the petty worries she had loaded on to John's shoulders, she felt ashamed. Dr Moir's remark, for instance, which had upset her, when he had run his finger along the dado saying, 'When was this last dusted?' He must have known that she was without help. She had explained to him how difficult it was to get a girl since they all wanted to work in the munitions factories. Also there was another time when he had asked her to keep Scott quiet during the surgeries. 'He never praises me,' she remembered saying, 'only picks faults.' Nor, when John was with the RAMC, did he ever tell her she could use the car. She thought the accident had rankled him.

'The taxi man was waiting for you?' Valerie asked, sitting down and accepting a drink from Scott.

'Yes, he was very nice.'

'Good. We employ him quite often, when we go to

parties and don't want to drive. How did you get to Toulouse for the plane?'

'By train. It's rather a long way for a taxi. The train is quite handy from Gramon.'

'Did someone drive you there?' Scott asked.

She felt ashamed that she didn't have a car. 'Yes, Boris drove me.'

'How are the Halliwells?'

'Fine. The house is within a week of being finished.'

'And Mr Graf, next door to them?'

'Didn't I tell you he died? He left his house to his nephew.'

'Have you met him?'

'Yes, and his wife and daughter and her baby.' That was all she was going to say. 'This must be boring for you?' She smiled at Valerie.

'Not at all. I'm lost in admiration that you are able to live there alone.'

'And I'm lost in admiration at the work you do.'

'Oh, that! My sisters have been much smarter than me. They're all in business. Two of them started a boutique in Dorchester, and the younger one is in the stock exchange. They all make far more money than I do.'

'You sound a very clever family.' Four girls, she thought. She remembered the three who had been bridesmaids. Perhaps the parents had gone on and on, hoping for a son. And then didn't want any more. Like John.

'I think we'd better get off. I've booked for eight,' Scott said.

She didn't think much of the restaurant, although she was assured by Scott it was very popular. Certainly there were a lot of smart young people there who laughed a lot.

She felt very much out of place. Perhaps she should start dyeing her hair.

Valerie seemed very interested in her life in Laborie. 'So you spend most of your time alone, Jane?'

'In a way. But it's surprising how you create a routine for yourself, and, of course, there's my writing.'

'Yes, of course. That's interesting. I've never understood how you do that. I want to write a book on paediatrics, but I don't have the concentration for it. I'd rather be working in the hospital, doing . . .'

'Perhaps you're too young. When I was busy in the practice I could never have contemplated writing. One needs time to think, and then if you're like me, who likes routine, I look forward to a stint each day.'

'You'll have to wait till you get the urge, darling,' Scott said. 'You're too busy accumulating knowledge just now.'

'You're right.'

'Do you know, Mother,' he said, 'she furnished your flat in no time at all, worked at it every evening until it was finished, wouldn't let me help. She applies herself to the job in hand. She's very creative.' He looked proud, which pleased Jane.

'You could tell that by the placing of the furniture, and the curtains are lovely, Valerie. Did you make the cushions to match for the sofa?'

'Yes, there was some stuff left over.'

'I'm very grateful to both of you.' Jane held out her hands across the table. 'I lived most of my life in a house I hated, now I have two I love. I'm so lucky.'

In bed that night she missed John very much. Perhaps it was the thought of Valerie and Scott in the same house which made her feel lonely, and she tested herself. Could she live with another man? No, she didn't think so. She couldn't contemplate living the rest of her life with a stranger after John. He had often said they had been made for each other.

She thought she had established a relationship with Valerie. It was the first chance she'd had to know her. Valerie had suggested that they meet at a pub for lunch near the hospital tomorrow. She was looking forward to that.

She was at the Westminster pub fifteen minutes before Valerie arrived. She breezed in, coat and hair flying, caught sight of Jane and sat down opposite her. 'So sorry! That bridge! Don't ever attempt to drive in London, Jane. Have you ordered?'

'No, I was waiting for you. How about some wine?'

'Good idea. White or red?'

'White, please. And it's on me, Valerie.' She had carefully placed a ten pound note in an accessible place in her handbag, and proffered it. Valerie waved it away.

'If you are intent on paying, I'll have them put it on the bill.'

'OK. What are you going to have?'

'I thought sandwiches. Does that suit you?'

'Yes. I'll leave you to choose.'

Valerie got up and went towards the bar. Better to leave her to do what's necessary, Jane thought. It's like being dropped into a different land. She looked around her at the other tables. What did they find to say? The volume of noise was deafening, and she compared it in her mind with the decorum at Pont l'Isle. Did the country you were in affect behaviour? Everybody in London seemed to live at high pressure. She had come by Tube, and had felt quite scared by the bustle, and how people pushed past her, looking ahead, making her feel like a visitor from another planet.

Valerie appeared, carrying two glasses of wine. 'They'll bring the sandwiches to us.'

'Good. How do you avoid stress living here? At Laborie it's so quiet, the pace of life slows down, that's what John liked particularly. He had to work so hard at Tynebay.'

'Is Scott like him?'

'No, I don't think so. John always seemed to be bursting with energy, everything he did showed that. I loved it when he came rushing upstairs to us when the surgeries were over. He laughed a lot, and when Scott was a baby, he would lift him and swing him around. And sometimes me! But as time went on and the practice took its toll, he became quieter.'

She didn't tell Valerie that she thought the back of their marriage had been broken when she found the letter. She would never forget his white face and his trembling voice. He had been the picture of a guilty man, and it had taken her a long time to realize that it shouldn't have mattered. He had died without her being able to tell him that, and she should have taken into account that his default was a measure of how much he had missed her.

'You look wistful, Jane,' Valerie said, smiling at her over her glass.

'Do I? That's been said to me before. How long do marriages last in London, Valerie?'

'I don't think London makes a difference. It depends upon the temperament of the couple, and if they went into it with the intention of making a go of it. Scott and I feel we're right for each other. Did you and his father feel the same?'

'Yes, oh, yes. But I never moved out of Tynebay on my own, and John went into the Army, so he had more opportunities of meeting other people. London must be the same.'

'Yes, I suppose so.' She looked up. 'Here are the sandwiches! I got a selection, roast beef, shrimps, cheese. Help yourself,' she said as they were put down before them.

'Thank you. I'll have shrimps, provided it leaves some for you.'

'I prefer the roast beef.' Valerie lifted a sandwich. 'Scott tells me that the senior doctor in the practice was a mean man.'

'Yes, that describes him. I've since wondered if his behaviour was influenced by his wife. Stella, she was called.'

'Did you know her?'

'Yes, she visited me when I was in a nursing home having Scott. An odd woman.'

'What do you mean?'

'She inferred she'd had a baby, Lucy, who had died. And yet she spoke sometimes as if she was there, as a little girl. She had bought a car, unbeknown to her husband, and she used to call and take me out if I could find someone to look after Scott. John was in the Army. We'd go to the cinema and then have tea in Gray Street, but her conversation was most peculiar, as if this Lucy was there. She said once that Lucy was jealous of Scott, and that was why she had asked me not to bring him. It was . . . spooky.'

'It certainly sounds spooky. Perhaps she was the cause of her husband's peculiar behaviour?'

'*Folie à deux* I called it, but now I'm not so sure.

120

Esther, the dispenser in the practice, knew them better than I did, and she said Stella was in and out of hospital. I think Dr Moir confided in her. He never said anything to John about his wife, although he might have been of some help. John was employed in a mental hospital before we went to Tynebay, and he said you got an odd feeling when dealing with the deranged. I said that sometimes Stella made my skin crawl, and he said that's because you can't understand her. It's funny, but when John was in the Army, I felt as if I was marooned with the Moirs, as if I needed some fresh air! I hadn't a friend to talk to, except Esther, who, when she talked about the Moirs, made me wonder if everyone around me was . . . odd. I even wondered if she and Dr Moir were having an affair.'

'He would certainly need a confidante. It sounds a most peculiar set-up.'

Jane nodded. 'Esther knew Stella called for me, in her car. I probably told her, and I said to her that I knew the Moirs had been in the house before us. She was cagey at first, then said they had, and told me that she and Stella had been quite friendly. When Stella became pregnant she asked her to go to Fenwicks with her to buy a maternity dress long before she needed it, and she began wearing her hair loose; it was generally done up. She became very peculiar, accusing her, or suggesting that she was trying to steal her husband. Then there was a terrible accident. In this house in Tynebay there was an iron staircase running down to the back yard and the garage. I was glad of that staircase because there was a platform at the top of it, and on Sundays, when I had to be in the house all day to answer the door and telephone, Esther being off duty, I used to put a chair there when

121

Scott was asleep and sit outside to get some fresh air. There was no garden. This staircase led to the garage in the yard. Stella had bought a Silver Cross pram, they were very popular then, upholstered like a car, and she kept it in the garage. Esther's dispensary looked on to the yard, and she said she often saw Stella coming down the iron staircase, going into the garage, taking out the pram and wheeling it round the yard. Esther told me a peculiar thing. A patient had told her she had seen Mrs Moir wheeling the empty pram outside in the street!'

'Poor soul!'

'Wait till you hear the end of it. On one of her trips to the garage, presumably, Stella's foot must have caught on this staircase, and Esther happened to look out of her window and saw her lying in the yard.' Valerie's head went up.

'How terrible!'

'Yes. Well, the upshot of it all was that she lost her baby, and her father, who was wealthy, bought them a house with a garden in Belsay and they moved there.'

'Sensible. I presume Esther summoned an ambulance, and so on when the accident occurred. Did Stella still bear any ill-will towards her?'

'No, I didn't get that impression. But I got the impression that Esther had supported Charles Moir during this debâcle. There may have been an affair then, but I don't think it lasted.'

'Well, that's some story,' Valerie said.

'There's more. It would take too long to tell. I'll write to you sometime and tell you about our experience with the Moirs.' She felt they were taking up too much of her time with Valerie. 'Our stay at Tynebay was fraught, and yet we couldn't move on. John was tired, he had those chesty colds . . .'

'You can get bedded down in a job and lose the initiative to move.'

'You're right. I felt Dr Moir resented me being there when John was in the Army. It was as if he felt I had to work my passage, earn my keep. Stella stopped, quite suddenly, calling for me, and I wondered if Dr Moir had found out that she had a car (she kept it in a garage nearby) and made her give it up. I sometimes think John and I got tainted by the peculiar atmosphere in the practice. Anyhow, we made the mistake of staying on after the war when we should have left. Although neither of us liked the place, we never got time to think or plan, besides John was popular, and he seemed to need that. The only positive thing we ever did was to buy the house at Laborie. We felt we returned to sanity there, and I'd hoped we would regain the relationship there we'd had at the beginning of our marriage.' She felt Valerie's eyes on her.

'And did you?

'I'm trying to convince myself that we did.' This was a bright girl.

Travelling back from London, Jane felt her visit had been a success. She had seen Valerie and Scott in operation, so to speak, and felt that they wouldn't make the same mistake as she and John had made. It was the difference between the two generations. She and John had been imbued with the same Scottish deference to authority, one didn't question it. While Valerie and Scott were free spirits and would plan their lives together, not allowing themselves to be influenced by any outside authority. It was a different marriage, a modern marriage.

In the train from Toulouse to Gramon, she was captivated again by the French landscape, and felt glad to be back again. It was a love affair, she thought, she didn't feel the same way about Scotland where she had been brought up, and where she had been restrained by old-fashioned tenets. It was something to do with the disposition of landscape, an aura, people fell in love with Tuscany as she had with south-west France. We are all Europeans, she thought, it's a question of being able to absorb a wider landscape. And again, London was for the young. She hadn't met anyone of her own age. In France she could be herself.

Trains were conducive to contemplation. She must write and tell Valerie about that terrible night when they had visited the Moirs. Then there was Rachel Green, who had come to the practice after Roger Mills had left. And Margo, a hysteric, if ever there was one. Strange how one's mind selected the high spots in one's past, and that night at the theatre had certainly been one. She could still feel the fear which had racked her and the guilt, as she had run home through the deserted streets.

Rachel had had no time for Dr Moir. 'What's his wife like?' she had asked. 'The atmosphere here is unhealthy, I felt it immediately.' And another time: 'I don't like the way Moir looks at me. Esther tells me his wife is round the bend.'

'Peculiar,' Jane had corrected her, objecting to Esther's description of Stella.

'He's asked me to stay on, but I've got my life planned out. I'm going to run a practice in Devon for the owner, a

124

lovely village, nice people around. This is a dump. I'm surprised you've stayed on.'

'So am I,' Jane had said.

In a rare bout of confidence she had told Rachel about her predecessor, Roger Mills, and that she had been attracted by him. 'You should have let yourself go,' Rachel had said. 'Everybody's doing it. Don't imagine that your John is keeping himself pure for you.'

She persuaded Jane to make up a foursome with her at the Royal Theatre. She had a friend who had four tickets, and although feeling dubious, she fixed up with Esther to act as babysitter for Scott. She was dressed and waiting for Rachel when she had finished surgery. They drove quickly into Newcastle and the theatre, where Rachel had arranged to meet her friend, James, and his friend, both officers home on leave.

For some time there had been a little sporadic bombing in the north-east, but no sooner were they seated between the two officers than there was the loud wail of the warning siren. The one on Jane's side put his hand on her arm when she made to get up. 'Wait!' he said. 'I expect the manager will make an announcement.' The man appeared at that moment in front of the curtains which had been drawn. 'Ladies and gentlemen,' he said, holding up his hands. 'I assure you, you are as safe here as in the street. It's our policy to carry on. There will be ten minutes' interval. Those who wish to leave should do so now.'

Jane turned to Rachel, clutching her arm. 'I must get home!' She heard the two officers laughing. 'She should be at the Front!' she heard the one called Bob say.

'I'm staying put,' Rachel shook off her hand. 'There won't be any transport, if you leave.'

'I know, but I'm worried about Scott.'

'You've no way of getting back on your own. Tell her, Bob.' He shrugged, and Jane remembered that he had made her blush when she had told him her husband was in Burma, and he had said, 'I see. So wifey is having a night out on the tiles.'

'I must go,' she said, and to Bob, 'excuse me, please.' He was forced to rise from his seat to let her pass and she heard Rachel complaining to her friend, James: 'I drove her here, but I'm not going to miss the show . . .'

Jane's head was buzzing. Scott, bombs falling on the house, Esther panicking. 'Excuse me,' she kept on saying, 'excuse me,' as she pushed her way along the row. You deserve this, she told herself, you believed Rachel when she told you it was time you had some fun, this is your punishment . . . She was at the door of the theatre, and she saw the street was deserted. Was she the only one who had qualms? But then they were all good at ignoring the war. They knew the drill.

There were no people waiting at the bus stop and she began to run. It was only two miles . . . She was stopped by an air-raid warden. 'Where are you heading for, miss?'

'I'm trying to get home.'

'Where's home?'

'Tynebay.'

'Take my advice,' he said, 'get into that shelter.' He pointed. 'When you hear the All Clear, there will be plenty of transport.'

'Thank you,' Jane said. No need to load him with her worry about Scott.

She broke into a run from time to time, then, when the pain in her side became unbearable, she would slow down to a walk. There were no people about, it was an eerie sensation to run through the quiet streets, with this panic in her breast, as if she was the only person in the world. She told herself that she was foolish to get into such a state, she didn't blame Rachel for not coming back with her, only reproached herself for falling in with her plans. She was Scott's guardian, and she had let him down. You should behave in the way which is natural to you, you should not fall in with other people's plans, she told herself, panting, as she ran.

When she got to the corner of her street, she took a deep breath, as she went round it. The house was still there, no sign of bomb damage! Would Esther have the sense to take Scott downstairs to the Morrison shelter in the waiting room? She reached the gate and opened it, ran up the steps leading to the front door and went in. As she did so, she heard a crash which didn't sound too far away, and went into the hall. 'Esther!' she called.

'In here!' It was Esther's voice coming from the waiting room.

She went in and crawled into the shelter, meeting Scott on all fours. She took him in her arms, crooning over him.

'He got a bit excited, so I've let him move around,' Esther said. She was in her nightdress and overcoat, and minus glasses. 'I can't see,' she said, peering. 'It *is* you, Jane?'

'Yes, I left the theatre. I got worried.'

'You wouldn't get a bus?'

'No, I ran home.' She had Scott in her arms, and he was clutching at her face. 'Yes, it's Mummy. I've run home to you, you warm little bundle.'

'There's the All Clear,' Esther said. 'You shouldn't have bothered.'

'Perhaps not. Come up and we'll have a cup of tea before you go home.' Esther had a beloved cat which she had to return to, she always insisted.

Over tea, Esther asked, 'Did Dr Green stay in the theatre?'

'Yes. She wasn't worried.'

'There were two blokes, weren't there? She told me. She's man mad! You should hear the stories she tells me about her conquests.'

'You shouldn't pay too much attention to what she tells you. I try not to.' It struck Jane that perhaps Esther minded not having a boyfriend. But what about Dr Moir? Hadn't Valerie remarked that perhaps he needed someone to confide in?

When she went to bed at one in the morning, after Esther had gone, Rachel hadn't come back. She thought she would try to stay awake to hear her, but the excitement of the night had been too much for her. Her mind was full of John. Was he behaving as Rachel had inferred? No, she assured herself, not my John. And as for Roger Mills, she would dismiss any lingering thoughts about him. Perhaps he'd had a girlfriend or wife? She hadn't thought that at the time, it was Rachel who had given her these ideas. Had he been interested in a spot of dalliance, nothing more?

'You were stupid running away,' Rachel said next morning at the kitchen table. 'We went on to a nightclub. Your man, Bob, got off with a girl there.'

'That doesn't concern me. I would never have forgiven myself if anything had happened to Scott.'

Rachel looked at her. 'Well, I never thought I'd meet anyone like you.'

You live and learn, Jane thought now, looking out at the Bouriane from the train window. She recognized the peaceful valley. It would soon be Gramon. And home.

Twelve

S he was busy at her Olivetti next morning. The visit to London, and particularly her conversation with Valerie, had supplied the necessary boost which she needed. Her thoughts were firmly centred on Tynebay. That had been evident to her in the train yesterday when she had remembered running home from the Newcastle theatre. With the memory, she had felt the same panic as she had felt then. 'O what a panic's in thy breastie!', she quoted from Burns as she typed.

That, of course, led on to the Moirs, and that tragic visit they had paid them.

It was while John was on leave, and before the letter. To their surprise they had been invited to the Moirs' house for dinner. 'He was quite pathetic.' John quoted Dr Moir: 'My wife would like you both to come and visit us. She's been away for some time, and wants to resume her normal life.'

Stella Moir telephoned Jane the following day. 'Charles wants me to start entertaining,' she said. 'Could you come to dinner on Friday?'

'Yes, we'd be delighted,' she answered. 'I'll arrange a babysitter for Scott.'

'No, no, I don't want you to do that,' she said. 'I thought it all out when I was . . . away. Scott and Lucy ought to get to know each other. I'll make up a bed for him with pillows on top of my bed, and you can always slip up from time to time and see how he is getting on.' She laughed, and that laugh had decided Jane. She made up her mind she wouldn't take Scott, and asked Esther if she would look after him. 'By the way,' she said, 'do you know if Mrs Moir has been away from home recently?' She thought Esther's freckles suddenly stood out on her pale cheeks.

'Why do you ask?' Esther said.

Jane shrugged her shoulders and replied, 'We've been asked to dinner. It's the first time. It's probably because John is home on leave.'

'Probably,' Esther said, avoiding Jane's eyes.

She told John later, saying that she was sure there was an affair going on between Esther and Dr Moir. 'She's so cagey.'

'Well, at least an understanding,' John said.

She and John set off, leaving Esther in charge. He agreed with her that they shouldn't take Scott. 'I'll say we thought it better to have Esther there to answer the telephone,' he said. 'That'll please old Moir. I rather think he may want to discuss my partnership.'

The house was reached by a long drive off the main road, and the trees surrounding it helped to deaden the noise of traffic. So John said. Creepy, she thought. She was full of trepidation as he rang the doorbell. It was opened by Dr Moir, his wife fluttering behind him. Their smiles seemed anxious.

'Come in, come in,' he said. 'This should have happened a long time ago. You two ladies know each other. This is my wife, Dr Maxwell.' Strange that he didn't use John's name, Jane thought, as she went forward to shake hands with Stella Moir.

131

The woman seemed to be in a high state of excitement. 'How nice, how nice,' she kept on saying. And then: 'Where's the baby, Jane? Didn't you bring him? Lucy will—'

'In here, please,' Dr Moir interrupted her, holding open a door. 'This room gives on to the garden. Stella is in charge of that.'

'Are you a keen gardener, Mrs Moir?' John asked. Jane saw her brighten.

'Oh, yes, we have a gardener, of course, but I always leave instructions . . .' She stopped suddenly. 'Drinks, Charles, then I'll excuse myself and go into the kitchen to see that all is going well.' She smiled round. 'Bessie, that's our help, put the joint in the oven for me, I just have to take it out at –' she consulted her watch – 'eight thirty. Wasn't that right, Charles?'

'I think so.' He waved his hand, 'You're in charge of the kitchen. A sherry, Mrs Maxwell?'

'Thank you.' It wasn't to be first names, then, she thought. And to his wife: 'Could I be of any assistance, Stella?'

'Goodness, no, you're the guest. I'll take mine with me, Charles,' she said. And then, looking at Jane: 'I'm disappointed in you, Jane, not bringing Scott. So will Lucy . . .' She stopped speaking suddenly.

Jane caught John's glance. He was listening to something Dr Moir was saying, his head inclined, but he must have overheard Stella's remark.

'Come and look at the view of the garden, Mrs Maxwell,' Dr Moir said, both men were standing at the French window,

'Yes, do that, Jane,' Stella Moir said in a perfectly normal voice.

The dinner was duly served, Dr Moir carving with much aplomb, Stella hovering with side dishes, and all seemed to be going well. We'll leave early, Jane thought. John was sitting opposite her, and she tried to signal her intention with her eyes.

After the fruit and cheese, Stella got up from her chair. 'Charles always makes the coffee, so this is a chance for you to come upstairs with me, Jane.'

'This is when the ladies retire,' John laughed. And Jane thought, he's trying to set her at ease.

Both men rose, and Jane followed Stella Moir out of the room.

At the top of the stairs she indicated the bathroom to Jane, and said, 'Come into my bedroom when you've finished, I've something to show you.'

What is wrong here? Jane asked herself, as she washed her hands. John would have noticed Stella's curious behaviour too. We must get away and talk it over. Is it as I said long ago to Rachel Green, a *folie à deux*, a chance expression which may have hit the nail on the head? At the top of the stairs she decided not to go into the room where Stella Moir was. She was afraid to be alone with her. Instead, she went downstairs again and into the dining room. John was sitting at the table alone.

She took her place opposite him, and they again exchanged glances. 'Dr Moir is making the coffee,' he said loudly, holding up his finger. She nodded. He might overhear their conversation. The kitchen led off the dining room.

'It's a lovely house,' she said.

'Yes, and a lovely garden. I'm glad we were here in time to catch a glimpse of it at least.'

Dr Moir appeared at the communicating door. 'I

133

overheard you discussing the garden. Take a walk around while I'm making the coffee. I see Stella isn't down yet.'

'I'd like that,' Jane said, and she and John got up.

In the garden they were free to talk. 'I don't like it here,' she said. 'She wanted me to go into the bedroom but I didn't go.'

'We'll leave as soon as we have coffee.' They were standing at a pool in the middle of the garden where they couldn't be heard.

'Has he said anything about the practice?'

'Not a word. He seems to be on edge all the time. My guess is that she's been in some sort of clinic, and this is his effort to lead a normal life.'

'Esther could tell us. It's still a peculiar set-up.'

'Well, you must admit, he's in a difficult position.'

'He should seek advice, or he could confide in you.'

'Not everyone does what they ought to do. Don't be hard, Jane.' She was to remember those words.

When they returned to the dining room, Dr Moir was esconsed with the coffee cups in front of him.

'Come along,' he said. 'Did you enjoy your tour, Mrs Maxwell?'

'Yes, thank you. The garden is a credit to your wife. We were admiring the lily pool.'

'Yes, Stella designed it. You can congratulate her when she comes down. Now, let's have coffee. We shan't wait for her.'

'Then we must go,' John said. 'Esther will be anxious to get away.'

Jane was looking across the table at him as he spoke. His crumpled white napkin was lying before him, and she noticed a pink stain on it. Had he spilled wine on it? So difficult to get out. Stella wouldn't be pleased. The thoughts were running through her mind, her eyes still on the napkin, when she distinctly saw another spot appearing on it.

'John!' She put her hand to her mouth. 'What are those spots on your napkin? They seem to be . . . appearing on it.' He lifted it, and looked above his head. So did she. She was aware of Dr Moir moving in his chair. There was a pause.

John's voice was husky. 'Doctor, what's above this room?'

The three of them had their eyes on the ceiling. There was a crack in it, and pink water was oozing through it. Jane saw another spot appear on the white napkin.

'My God!' Charles Moir got up. 'It's the bathroom! What can it be?' He made for the door.

John hurriedly got to his feet. 'I'm coming with you!' he said. They both dashed from the room, and Jane, stunned, sat for a moment before she got up too and followed them upstairs.

She heard Moir's voice on the upstairs landing. 'I noticed the water was running cold in the kitchen.' His voice was strangled. 'What has she done? Is it locked, doctor?'

Jane got to the landing just in time to see John putting his shoulder to the bathroom door. He half fell in. Dr Moir was close behind him, and she followed them inside, feeling the wetness of the tiles through her thin slippers.

She could scarcely bring herself to look, to turn her head in the direction of the bath. When she did, she saw Stella Moir floating in the pink water, her hair spread out round her like seaweed.

'Stella!' Dr Moir was kneeling at the side of the bath, stroking her face. 'Oh, what have you done? Oh, my God,' he groaned, looking up at John. 'They warned me, they warned me . . .'

John bent over him. 'You must help me to get her out, doctor,' he said. His voice was infinitely gentle. 'Jane,' he said, over his shoulder, 'could you get a blanket from somewhere?'

'Yes, all right!' She was glad to be given something to do, to get away. She dashed along the corridor, the memory of Stella's face with the floating hair round it like a mirage in front of her. She passed a half-open door, and had a confused view of flying figures on the walls. She reached the bedroom which Stella had indicated earlier, and once in, went towards the bed. There were pink shaded lights on either side of it. In the middle of the counterpane there was an arrangement of pillows, like a nest, and lying beside it was a chiffon scarf. She remembered Stella Moir had worn one like it when she had visited her in hospital, red, floating. The sight of it, and its possible implication galvanized her into action. She stripped the bed, tossing aside the pillows, the counterpane, the sheets, until she came across a blanket, and pulling it free, rolled it into a bundle and ran out of the room with it under her arm.

In the bathroom she saw they had managed to lift Stella on to the floor. John was bending over her, obviously trying to resuscitate her. Her eyes were wide open, as if in submission, and Dr Moir was sitting on the bathroom stool, his head in his hands. He looked up as Jane came in.

'She's gone,' he said. 'My Stella's gone. It's all my fault . . .' He put his head in his hands again.

136

She went to him, and put her hand on his shoulder, then finding nothing to say, knelt down beside John with the blanket. 'Do you want this under her?' she asked. She was stiff with shock, trying to avert her eyes, not succeeding.

He looked up. 'Not now. I'd thought at first . . . Never mind.' He took it from her, and placed it gently over Stella Moir's body. 'I was thinking we might roll her in it, but . . .'

'She's dead?' she whispered the word.

He nodded, getting up and going to Dr Moir. He bent over him, his hand on his shoulder and said, 'Come on, doctor, we'll get you downstairs and phone . . .' He turned his head and spoke under his breath to Jane, 'We'll have to dial 999.'

Walking behind them, she listened to him speaking to Dr Moir. 'It's a terrible shock for you. We'll get you a whisky, then I'll phone your doctor.'

That's it, she thought. John is good at this.

Downstairs, he asked Dr Moir if there was anyone he would like to send for. Whisky in hand, the man looked up, his glance scarcely focusing on him. 'Who is your doctor?' John repeated.

'Yes,' he said after a pause, 'we'd better have Dr Lenzie from the village. And Stella's father, Reg Buxton. He lives in Newcastle, Whiteley Gardens. What is the number, now? Oh, I know, 26. He'll be devastated!'

John went out, and Jane was left with Dr Moir. What did one say, what could one say? Except: 'I'm so sorry. What a terrible shock for you.'

'Poor Stella,' he said, 'You don't know . . .' They sat in silence until John came back.

'The doctor and your father-in-law are on their way,' he said. 'Will Mr Buxton be able to stay with you?'

Moir nodded. 'Widower, lives alone. Fond of . . . Stella.' He put his head in his hands, and Jane, looking at him, felt nothing but pity for the man, and a feeling that she might have been misjudging him. There was nothing more they could do for the poor soul. When the ambulance arrived, and shortly after, the doctor, they left. They hadn't met Mr Buxton. John had assured Dr Moir that he would look after the practice, he still had a week to go of his leave. In the car they scarcely spoke for the first ten minutes.

Jane broke the silence first. 'Do you know, John, when I passed an open door on the landing I could see that it was a child's room, with a Peter Pan motif on the wallpaper. I saw Wendy and Peter flying, and the Lost Boys . . .'

'Tragic.'

'Another thing, there was a kind of nest of pillows on top of their bed. And a scarf lying beside it. Stella's. What if . . .'

'Don't go any further. The woman's dead, and we now know what he's had to put up with for so long. He could have got help. But there are some people who still regard mental illness as a shameful thing . . .'

'No lectures, please.'

Thirteen

1971

Boris had called last night to remind her of the Mechoui, and they had talked for some time. She had been glad of the interruption. Her nerves were jangling with memories.

They were in the *salon* where she had set up her typewriter, a pleasant room with a table which she rarely used, preferring to eat in the kitchen. Boris had thrown himself into an easy chair at the window. 'You look agitated,' he said.

She was. She felt she had to take her mind off the Moirs. 'What's your favourite place around here?' she asked him. When he said he would like notice of that question, she said, 'I'm thinking peace. And that means the Causse. When it was too hot, John and I used to take ourselves off up there. We'd find a patch of grass free of those stones which come through the soil, its bones, and lie flat on our backs staring at the sky. We'd choose a spot where there was a hedge of scrub oak and juniper and use it as a windbreak. You know what the wind is like up there. There would be the scent of thyme and lavender and the sound of larks, and we'd follow the flight of a hawk, as it sailed against that lovely harebell blue sky.'

Her voice broke, and Boris had got up and put an arm round her shoulders, pulling her against him. 'You're working too hard. You're right. It *is* another world up there, two worlds in fact, the teeming insect world, and your world.'

'And the world in the sky, the hawk's world,' she said. 'He's king of that one. I don't know why I'm crying. Yes, I do.'

'Does you good,' he said.

Hazel was the type of woman who didn't relinquish the front seat, either through lack of sensitivity, i.e. manners, or the wish to emphasize her station as wife. That's your cynicism again, she thought of herself. Hazel hasn't given it a thought, or perhaps she gets like me, queasy in the back.

She leant forward, her elbows on the back of Hazel's seat. 'I'm looking forward to the Mechoui,' she said. 'John and I always went.'

'Good. Boris says this is how to integrate, and I know some people in the hotel who are turning up.'

'Visitors?'

'Yes, from Canterbury. Rather boring, but they were keen to go and I said I would meet them.'

'Hazel thought we shouldn't go to the Pont l'Isle first,' Boris said, 'that we should have to ask them to join us. We'll do it another time.'

'It's just that I don't want to encourage them too much,' Hazel said. 'They're rather pushy, and we'd be landed with them all night.'

Jane decided not to comment. She loved village gatherings. And she remembered many of them. They reminded her of a Bruegel painting. Scott had been taken when he was young, and she remembered him being too shy to play with the village children, and sitting on her knee most of the time. John had tried to persuade him, but it had been no good. Scott felt out of place, because he didn't understand what the children said. She had known that was the reason for his reluctance, and she had tried to teach him a few useful phrases, but the truth of it was that as he grew up he had never taken to France as they had, thought that where they had decided to settle was too quiet, and preferred to go to Italy with a friend whose parents had a house in Tuscany.

He had always had a taste for the high life and had acquired a snobbishness which she couldn't understand. She wondered if it was because the children at Tynebay had a Tyneside accent and he had been critical of that.

When they arrived at St. Martin there was the strong smell of meat cooking on the barbecue, the meat supplied by Monsieur Gaillard, as she knew. The table was set in the main street, and the village women were scurrying around putting the finishing touches to it. She recognized Madame Desirée, the butcher's wife, very important with a high hairdo and dangling earrings, and minus her white coat which had been superseded with a frilly apron over a print dress, very decolleté. She caught sight of the three of them and rushed forward to greet them, like an ambassadress.

'*Bonsoir, mesdames et monsieur, suivez-moi, s'il vous plaît.*' They were placed beside the Lisieux family. This must be the Laborie contingent, Jane thought. Benoit and his wife greeted them with pleasure, saying that Agnès and her husband would be along soon, as they were helping behind the scenes. Madame Lisieux had her grandchild on her knee.

141

The Remy Boys were already playing on the platform and the children were running about around their feet. Some of them were attempting to dance the polka, which was the favourite with the band and the dancers, Jane remembered.

Monsieur Gaillard, who was also the mayor, was on the platform making his speech of welcome, the children had been shooed off, and they were soon flocking about the table like birds looking for titbits. When Monsieur Gaillard had finished and been duly applauded, the village women began to circulate with huge plates of food and the Mechoui was soon in full swing with the Remy Boys providing a musical background. Jane noticed that the Remy Boys had aged since she last saw them, in fact their title was a misnomer, and knew that if John had been there he would have whispered something in her ear which would have made her laugh.

She looked around at the people, talking, laughing, eating, the children dressed in their finery, a rural picture. Why had it not appealed to Scott? Everybody seemed to be in fine form, there was a great deal of laughter, children crying, people from outlying villages greeting those they knew here.

'And a good time is being had by all,' Boris said, sitting beside her. 'It's the highlight of the year.' He repeated his remark in French to Madame Lisieux.

'*C'est ça*,' she agreed. 'Agnès met her husband at the Mechoui, *il a deux ans*.'

'*Un marriage marché?*' He nodded.

'They have a lovely baby,' Jane leant forward and took the baby's hand, and thought how beautiful they are when young, that wide-eyed innocence. '*Comme elle est belle*,' she said, and Madame Lisieux nodded.

'*Elle est mignonne*. Guy would have liked a boy, but there is plenty of time. They will inherit the farm, and a son is needed.'

'*Je comprends. La petite, elle a peur du feu d'artifice?*'

'*Je ne sais pas. C'est sa première visite.*'

'*Le Mechoui c'est comme le* "coming-out" in England for girls,' Jane said, letting herself in for some explanation.

Hazel, who had been looking anxiously around, suddenly said, 'There they are!' and stood up, waving. Jane looking in the same direction, saw a smartly-dressed couple coming towards them. Hazel introduced them, 'Tim and Laura Fraser.' There were mutual greetings, Boris introducing the farmer and his wife. Jane noticed Laura Fraser's disdainful air.

'Where shall we sit? Are those two seats taken?' she said, pointing to two empty ones beside Madame Lisieux.

Jane was just going to say, yes, they are, but Boris was asking Benoit in his fluent half-French, if the Frasers might occupy the two vacant seats, and Benoit was waving his arms in obvious agreement.

'He says Agnès and Guy must be with their young friends,' Boris said. 'We can have their seats.'

Madame Benoit said to Jane, '*Typique!* Gran'mère is left with the baby.'

'*Les voici*,' Jane said. She had been looking around and saw the young couple coming towards them.

Agnès made for the baby, and lifted her from her mother's lap. She glanced at Hazel's friends, ensconced in their seats, then at her mother, taking in the situation. '*Nos reviendrons à nos amis, Maman*,' she said. The Frasers seemed oblivious.

143

Boris was apologizing. Jane marvelled again at how he managed with his half-French to make himself understood. It must be his smile. She saw the Frasers busily talking with Hazel, unaware that they had commandeered Agnès' and Guy's seats.

When they all had finished eating they remained in their seats, watching the dancing, and Jane was surprised when Benoit asked her to dance. She noticed Boris had bowed to his wife, probably to break up the conversation between her and her two friends.

There was a great deal of greetings on the floor, and it seemed to be the custom of the men to interrupt a couple and exchange partners, which she remembered. 'Perpetual Excuse Me' she had called it. The shop owners paid their respects by dancing with her: Monsieur Gaillard, Monsieur Gitang, perhaps to assure themselves of her continued custom, and then Tim Fraser, who proved quite an interesting man when separated from his wife. They had come home from Zambia, and in answer to her questions he gave her much information. She was listening with interest to his description of the country and the wild life when she heard someone say, 'Excuse me,' and she found herself in the arms of Jan Graf.

'Are you here with your wife?' she asked him. It was the first thing she could think of.

'No,' he said. 'She decided to stay in Amsterdam. We have agreed to divorce.'

'Oh, I'm so sorry. Did little Rosabel get better?'

'It's nothing to do with Rosabel.'

'I didn't mean . . .'

'I'm sure you didn't. No, the baby was quite well when I saw her last, with her mother. I'll tell you the reason later why Bella and I are splitting up.'

144

'There's no obligation . . . nor is it any of my business.'

'You're here with Boris and Hazel?' He ignored her remark.

'Yes.'

'Perhaps they'll let me run you home.'

Jane didn't reply. She wasn't sure that she wanted any of Jan Graf's confidences, nor to be driven by him again.

She changed the subject and told him of her trip to London, then he escorted her back to her seat. The table was deserted. He sat down beside her. 'Do you like the Mechoui?' he asked, obviously not intending to leave her.

'I've always liked them. I feel part of the countryside. I'm not an urban type, although now that I have a pied-à-terre in London . . .'

'My flat is on a canal in Amsterdam. Not far from Anne Frank's house. I needed a town address. We have a house in the country. Bella occupies it.'

'I see.' That was all she was going to permit herself to say.

Boris came back to the table with Hazel, 'Well,' he said, looking surprised when he saw Jan. 'You're like Houdini, Jan. When did you arrive?'

'An hour ago. I went to the farm for milk, and the man there told me that everybody was at the Mechoui. He was Benoit's brother, I believe, from Cahors, and he had driven over to look after things for Benoit. So I made myself some coffee back home and decided to come here, hoping I might get something to eat.'

'If you can charm Madame Gaillard . . .' The lady in question came bustling over.

'Is there any food left, Madame, for my neighbour?' Boris asked.

She gave Jan an appreciative glance. 'I think I could manage to find you something, monsieur.' She went off. Jane noticed how the two men's eyes followed her.

After he had eaten, Jan didn't monopolize her. She saw him dancing with Madame Gaillard, Hazel, and Laura Fraser as the night wore on. After the fireworks, and the small bustle while the children were taken home, the last dance was announced, and he came to where she was sitting with Madame Lisieux. 'May I?' he said, bowing, and she got up smiling, saying good-bye to Madame Lisieux, and walked with him to the platform.

'At least you got a meal by coming to the Mechoui,' she said.

'That was not my only purpose,' he looked at her. They waited until they saw a space in the dancers whirling past then joined them on the platform.

She thought, What an enigmatic man he is. The memory of him kissing her was strong in her mind, making her feel uncomfortable with him. He held her closely, but didn't speak. What shall I say when he asks again if he can run me home? she thought. Shall I say that since Boris brought me, I feel I should go back with him, and thought again, no, that won't do. She wished he wouldn't hold her so closely, and wondered if he was presuming on the kiss.

Thoughts were going round in circles in her mind when the music stopped, with a roll of drums, and the dancers stood in a circle with arms crossed and hands linked, the usual end to the Mechoui. The Marseillaise was played by the band. 'That's it,' she said to Jan, and he looked down at her, smiling.

They came down from the platform and met Hazel and

Boris. 'Would you lend me Jane for company back?' Jan asked him.

'How do you know I want to go with you?' she said, laughing, but annoyed at his presumption.

'Oh, I'm sorry, I shouldn't have presumed.' He smiled.

'If it's only company you want,' Hazel said. 'I'll go with you.'

He looked taken aback, then said to Boris, 'Sure you don't mind?'

Jane saw the annoyance in Boris' eyes, and wondered if he and Hazel had been quarrelling, and this was her way of getting back at him. 'Suits me,' he said. 'Come along, Jane, we'll race them back.'

'Let's make it exciting and go back by the N20. What do you say, Boris?' Jan said.

Jane looked at Boris, doubtfully. He had been drinking, and so had Jan. Men, she thought.

'Sure,' he said. 'If you want some fun, I'm with you.' Hazel didn't protest.

Jane walked back with Boris to his car, and got in beside him. 'What made you agree with Jan?' she asked him.

'Well, in the hope of bringing him down a peg or two. He fancies himself as a driver. Do you mind?'

'No,' she said, thinking, Why am I lying, of course I mind.

He drove carefully through the village, avoiding the groups of people walking home from the Mechoui, then along the road for five minutes where he took a right turn. She was pacified.

'Can you see them?' he asked.

'That could be his car behind us.' As she spoke the car she had seen made up on them and flashed past.

'He's a cocky bugger, isn't he? Boris said.

'Are you sure it was them?'

'Positive. It was an Aston Martin.'

'Now they'll be back before us.'

''Fraid so. Maybe they'll be held up at the junction. It's a busy one.'

When they got to the junction there was no sign of another car, and they had to wait for a few minutes before they got on to the N20.

'Now it's a straight run home and then the lane to our house,' Boris said. 'We may make up on them.'

The road took a slight bend and when they drove round it, the autoroute ahead of them was deserted.

'Where have they got to?' Jane said, surprised.

'Goodness knows, unless he decided to take the turning past ours and still arrive before us.'

'But why?'

'To show off. Why ask?'

Jan would have to drive very fast to arrive at the hamlet before them, she thought, if that were the case. She wondered if Boris was getting rattled, but decided not to comment. How stupid men were, she thought, anything for a dare. She had a feeling of unease.

There were no lights on in the houses in the hamlet. It looked very peaceful, illuminated by the moon behind the clouds, which were edged by silver. Like the calm before a storm, she thought. The trees were stencilled against the pale sky, the road shone in the darkness.

'No sign of life,' Boris said. 'Would you like me to drive you home, Jane?'

As he spoke there was the sound of a car engine, and in a second or two a car appeared, drove up to them, and stopped. A policeman put his head out of the window.

'Does a Mr Jan Graf live here? Owner of an Aston Martin?'

'Yes,' Boris said. 'Why do you ask?'

'There's been a crash. The car's in a ditch in the lane above here. The farmer there alerted me. I live near him.'

'In the name of God!' Boris said. 'What's happened to those inside?' Jane held her breath.

'My mate is there,' the policeman said. 'We've sent for lifting equipment. There are two people in it, who we can't get out. I came along to verify if it was Mr Graf. We recognized the car. Is he in?'

'No. He's in the car. With my wife!' He turned a horrified face to Jane.

'You go back with the policeman, Boris,' Jane said. She saw he was shaking. So was she.

'I'm sorry to bring such bad news,' the policeman said. 'Come along, sir. They may have got them out by this time. We saw the woman waving . . . your wife.'

'Oh, God!'

'On you go, Boris,' Jane said, putting her arms round him. 'Don't despair. It may turn out to be all right.'

'Yes, come along, sir,' the policeman said.

Jane sat in Boris' car when they had gone, until she couldn't bear it any longer. She wondered if she should alert anyone in the hamlet, the Croziers or the Lamartines. After a time she heard the noise of a car and saw it turn into the Lisieux's farm. They would be returning from the Mechoui, she thought. I must let them know. Boris had left the keys in the car.

Her legs felt useless. She needed to tell the Lisieux, she needed company. She turned the key in the lock, put the car into gear and drove off. It was simple, it was easy. Now, could she stop? She put her foot on the brake. Yes.

149

She saw Benoit walking towards her from his barn. He opened the car door on her side, and she tried to speak.

'What is wrong, Madame Maxwell?' he asked.

Her voice wouldn't come at first. She cleared her throat and then was able to tell him. 'An accident, Benoit. Near your neighbour, up on the hill . . .'

'Monsieur Lucien?'

'Mr Graf's car is in the ditch there. He's in it with Madame Halliwell.' Benoit's face registered puzzlement. 'A policeman took Mr Halliwell back with him. Just now. I think I'll drive there and see if I can be of any help. Would you like to come with me.?'

Madame Lisieux was standing beside them. He turned to her. 'An accident, chérie. Monsieur Graf and Madame Halliwell.' He put an arm round her shoulders.

'*Mon Dieu!* You go, Benoit. Come with me, Madame.'

'No, thanks. I must help Monsieur Halliwell. He'll be terribly distressed.'

'Let us go, then,' Benoit said. He got in beside Jane. Everyone seemed to have forgotten that she didn't drive. Once again, she turned the key in the lock, let the brake off, and the car moved steadily forward, her hand on the gear.

'Turn here,' he said after a few minutes. 'Slowly, there's a truck in the road.' It was the lifting apparatus. She saw Boris standing in the road, got out and ran towards him. He turned an anguished face to her.

'They're cutting the roof off. They didn't want me there.'

'Of course not. Here's Benoit. I brought him.'

'My dear sir,' Benoit put his hand on Boris' shoulder. 'You go back with Madame Maxwell, and I'll stay here with Lucien.' Another man had joined them, thin, dark-haired.

'Terrible business, Benoit. We had just gone to bed . . .'

'Yes, a shock. I'll come to your caravan, Monsieur Halliwell, as quickly as possible, and give you the news whenever they get them out.'

'No,' Boris said. 'I'd rather wait and see if I can be of any use . . .'

'All right,' Jane said, seeing his distress. 'Come and sit in the car. They'll let you know . . .' He allowed himself to be led towards it.

Benoit walked towards the lifting truck and she could see him and Monsieur Lucien standing watching and talking together. She now saw an ambulance arriving and park beside the truck, saw stretchers, saw bodies being lifted from the car and laid on the stretchers. She tried talking to Boris who had his face in his hands. 'I'll drive you back now, Boris, the police or Benoit will come and tell us.' He nodded, not raising his head.

It was the following day. She had left Boris in his caravan after staying with him for some time with Benoit who had walked back to tell Boris that the ambulance men had said both were alive. Boris was distraught, blaming himself for the accident. 'I was showing off, just showing off,' he kept on repeating. She couldn't take any more. When the doctor came, she left. The fear which had clutched her heart had left her, and in its place was a deep sadness. She would have to walk down later and see Boris, she told herself when she arrived at her house. At that moment she heard the noise of a car and Benoit got out. She had collapsed on a seat in the *bolet* and she got up and ran down the steps to meet him. 'What's the news, Benoit?' she said. His brown face was lined, and she saw his heavy moustache was trembling.

'The worst possible news, Madame. Neither of them have survived. Mrs Halliwell rallied for a time, but died this morning. The doctor took Boris into hospital. He's to be sedated, and kept in for a day or so.'

'That's wise. Poor soul, it's too much to bear.'

'I've to take you to my wife, and you must join us for a meal. Last night I thought you were going to faint any minute.'

'That's why I left. But you've been so good. I don't know of any friends or relatives they might have who should be told.'

'There were the two friends at the Mechoui, Mr and Mrs Fraser. And Boris will be able to give addresses in a day or so.'

The next few days were difficult to get through. She walked to St. Martin and told the Frasers, and they turned out to be very helpful, driving her about wherever she wanted to go. Boris was kept at the Gramon Hospital, then allowed to get up for the funeral, which Benoit arranged for them. The young priest at the St. Martin church proved very helpful to Boris, and was often closeted with him in the caravan.

Mrs Graf had been notified and later a friend of hers had telephoned and said he had made arrangements for Jan's body to be transported to Amsterdam, where he would be buried in the family plot. She would come later to Laborie and make arrangements for the house to be sold. Her daughter had no desire to live there. Jane wondered if the friend was Jan's replacement, and the reason for the divorce. She would never know.

As for Boris, he would need all her support, and she did her best. As it happened the builders had arrived to complete the house, and he was occupied in giving them instructions, which filled his time. She herself was planning to go to London and stay in her flat. She had telephoned Scott and told him what had happened.

How things could change from one day to the next, she thought, and her memory returned to the past as a relief. She was unable to write, but sat for long hours in the *bolet*, her mind full, and thinking of how she had dealt with the present crisis, compared with that young girl in Tynebay.

She remained in Laborie to attend Hazel's funeral with Boris. He was still profoundly shocked, but calm. He had arranged for Hazel to be buried in the cemetery at St. Martin. 'I want her close by me,' he said. 'Her relatives wanted her buried at Golder's Green, but I refused. She had said she would live here, and therefore I feel I should remain in the house now that it's finished.'

Father Anthony, the young priest at St. Martin, told her not to worry about Boris, that he would keep an eye on him.

Going back in the train and plane to London, the ache in her heart reminded her of the pain in her side she had felt when she was running through the deserted streets of Newcastle with the sirens sounding around her. Guilt.

Fourteen

1945

'Daddy's coming home today,' she told Scott who was sitting on the carpet playing with his bricks. 'What are you going to say to him?'

'Hello, Daddy,' he said, balancing a red one on top of a blue one. 'I did it!'

'Good!' John would be impressed by how well he spoke. Three years since he had seen him, before he went to Burma, after that fateful evening at the Moirs' house. 'Come and we'll go to the window and look for him.' Jane lifted him in her arms. What a weight he was. John would get a surprise, compared with the baby he left.

They had been standing waiting for five minutes only when she saw the taxi draw up and John get out, carrying a kit bag. He looked up, caught sight of them, and waved.

She heard the door open, then his steps as he ran upstairs. She was shaking with excitement. She put Scott down and taking him by the hand, walked to the top of the stairs. 'Hello!' she said as they met. 'You're earlier than I thought.'

'Do you want me to go back?' She couldn't believe she was seeing that smile again.

154

'Of course not.' She laughed, and he swept her into his arms and swung her round.

'Hello, Daddy,' Scott said. He was standing beside them.

'Hello!' John bent down and picked him up and with both of them in his arms waltzed down the corridor towards the bedroom. He put Scott down, then pulled Jane on to the bed. 'The same old place!'

'You'll make Scott jealous,' she said looking up at him. How handsome he was! 'Let's go into the sitting room and he can play with his bricks there. Tell Daddy what you're building, Scott.'

'A castle. Come and see.' He caught hold of John's jacket and pulled.

'Just a moment till I kiss Mummy, old son.' He bent over Jane. 'You're more beautiful than I remembered, but thinner.'

'The rations aren't so good.' Hers often went to Scott. 'All the food goes to the forces.'

'Don't you believe that. We got lots of cigarettes dropped. It was a question of smoking rather than eating. I'm now a confirmed smoker.'

'What a pity.'

She got up, brushing away his clinging hand. Laughing. She couldn't stop it. 'Come on. Later. Take his hand.' She had seen the look on Scott's face. 'Remember, he's not used to having a daddy around.'

'Come along, Scott.' He lifted him in his arms, and they went into the sitting room together. 'The same old place,' he said, looking around.

'I've got tea ready,' she said. 'I'll go and get the tray.' She couldn't believe she was so shy with him.

John nodded. He was listening intently to some story

155

Scott was telling him. 'How well he talks,' he said to her. She was at the door.

In the kitchen she looked at her face in the mirror at the window. 'He's back!' she said to her reflection. 'It's true, true, true!' When she went into the sitting room with the tray, she saw he was on the floor with Scott, helping him to build a castle with the bricks. He looked up and saw her, and jumped to his feet.

'Let me take that, darling.' He took the tray from her. Roger Mills used to do the same thing, she remembered, but, then, he hadn't called her 'darling'.

They spent the evening talking. 'How's Moir since he married?' he asked.

'Not much different, which proves something, I don't know what. I believe she's a nurse. I told you Esther left, didn't I?'

'Yes, she's another casualty. Did she ever confide in you?'

'No, she didn't, but she looked terrible. We'll leave, John, now that you're home. This was a bad choice for us. He's a cold man, unapproachable.'

'I agree. We'll start looking around. Don't let's talk about it now.'

'But we'll make plans,' she said. 'I'm sorry. I shouldn't have raised the subject, the minute you're home. Tell me about Burma.' She listened to his description of the forests and the rivers, the monsoons, the heat when sweat dropped from your forehead on to the page. He had described it in his letters. He showed her photographs, some were groups, in all of them there was a dark-haired girl with dark eyes sitting beside him. 'Who's that?' she said, pointing.

'They grouped the doctors together. Dr Choompal,

156

Ravella. Very popular. We all went on a houseboat to Srinagar. Gosh, Jane, you would have loved it. The moon was like a water melon.'

'Sounds very romantic.' Srinagar, she thought. My shawl.

'Don't get me wrong.' He got up and sat beside her on the sofa, put his arm round her and kissed her cheek. 'There were about twenty of us there. My first leave.'

'I rarely went anywhere.' She heard the whine in her voice. 'Once, a woman doctor who was here, took me to the theatre in Newcastle, but when the siren went, I was so worried about Scott that I ran the whole way home.'

'Poor you! I can understand that. You were always such a conscientious wee soul. Was the bombing bad here?'

'Not bad. But Dr Moir . . . I've given up trying to understand him. When he came back after Stella's suicide, he was still "distant", as we used to say in Scotland. Which made me think that, well, there were faults on both sides of that marriage. I used to lie in bed and try to work it out. Was he to blame for her state of mind? He's certainly petty, and cold, and I think Esther found that out, and that's why she left. Perhaps she was hoping he would marry her. It would take a psychologist to get to the bottom of what went on.' She shouldn't talk like this on his first night home. He didn't mind Moir as much as she did, he'd been out of it while she was left here, plenty of company obviously, while she'd had none except the doctors who had been here.

Dr Ravella Choompal. The name came into her mind. Be sensible, Jane. Would he have mentioned her if he had been involved with her? It's Rachel Green who put such ideas into your head.

'Did you have many doctors staying here?' he asked.

157

'Two who stayed for two weeks, each. A man and a woman. Others who didn't stay. I told you in my letters.'

'Didn't you object?'

'I felt it might jeopardize your future if I did.'

'You shouldn't let yourself be put upon, you've always been like that. I've learned to speak out in the Army. You should hear me tearing a strip off my batman.'

'You've changed.' She laughed at him. He looked older and leaner, and with a bravado which she didn't recognize. 'I haven't. I should have been in the Army too.'

'You wouldn't have liked it. I didn't tell you much in order not to distress you. The slaughter, and the weather made it worse, mud, monsoons, and the poverty of the people. The children were adorable, grateful for anything. You make up your mind never to complain again. When we crossed into Arakan and took part in the action at Nyakdank Pass, and then we were in the Admin Box . . . well, I told you about that. Where my CO was killed. Getting to Rangoon was like the end of a nightmare. It's a wonderful city. I put in there for discharge.'

'I'm sorry I complained about Dr Moir.'

'No, you've had your own war. We'll discuss everything later. Let's just enjoy tonight, OK? This cake's good. Did you bake it?'

They played with Scott until his bedtime, then they gave him his bath. While she made supper he went downstairs to see Dr Moir. When he came back he said, 'You're right. He hasn't changed. It's as if we hadn't been there when his wife cut her wrists. "So you're back, Dr Maxwell." Cold as charity.'

'But I'm not.' She turned from the stove and put her arms round his neck. She had a wooden spoon in her hand.

'Look out! You're ruining my uniform.' He lifted a cloth and wiped at a spot on his collar.

'Oh, sorry! Never mind. We'll get it cleaned. I'll take it tomorrow. Then we'll pack it away as an heirloom.'

'Good idea.'

'Are you going to find it dull to be home and working here?'

'Dull with you and Scott? He looked down on her. 'Not likely!'

'With no Dr Choompal?' The words slipped out.

'Don't harp on, Jane.' He pulled away. 'I shouldn't have shown you these photographs.'

'I'm sorry.' But she felt very ordinary beside the exotic-looking doctor with the exotic name. 'I shouldn't have said that. I think my nerves are on edge.'

'Yes, I know. Give me time to have a talk with Moir. We won't leave him in the lurch, but we'll start looking around for another practice. We must have somewhere to go.'

'All right. Oh, John, it's lovely to have you back.' She put her arms round his neck again. 'No decisions to be made alone, but I'm sure we should definitely get away from here. Tynebay's a dull place, in any case.'

He nodded. 'Any place would be dull.'

'After Burma?'

'Well, it's the excitement, and the moving on all the time. Of course, I saw some terrible sights, but I don't want to think about that. The main thing is that we're together again.'

I hope that will be enough, she thought.

She was in bed when he came into the room. 'I've folded the uniform and left it in the bathroom,' he said.

159

'OK. What have you got on under that dressing gown?' she said, putting on a severe look.

'Nothing. I haven't unpacked yet.'

'Well, I'm not going to be your batman. Find your own pyjamas.'

'Why bother?' he jumped into bed beside her.

The same old John, she thought, like a boy. And later his face was wet, and he said, 'Oh, wife, it's good to be back with you. How I missed you!'

'I missed you, but I had Scott. Don't you think he's a fine little boy?'

'He's a credit to you. I don't feel like a father just now. I think it has to grow by proximity. But it'll come. At the moment I just want you.'

No one used the speaking tube that night. John thought the news must have got round that the young doctor was home. But he was up at eight, and brought her a cup of tea, then went dutifully downstairs. She had never been able to get rid of the feeling that he was playing at being the breadwinner. She felt far more responsible for Scott and the running of the practice, and for him. He was a true Peter Pan.

After he went down to the surgery, and she had fed Scott, she went into the bathroom and saw the uniform neatly folded. 'Daddy?' Scott said, pointing.

'Yes. We're going to go out with the go-chair this morning and take Daddy's suit to the dry cleaners.' She had got into the habit of speaking to him like an adult, for want of company. She was going through the pockets as she spoke. Her hand touched a folded piece of paper, and she drew it out and unfolded it.

'A letter,' she said to Scott.

'Daddy's?'

160

'Daddy's letter.' She was opening it, she was reading it, and the words were jumping at her, blinding her.

'*Darling, you were so amusing last night, I laughed till I cried . . .*'

'A letter,' she said to Scott. She sat down on the bathroom stool and went on reading. '*Wasn't the moon huge, like a water melon . . .*'

She looked up and met John's eyes. He was standing at the door.

'Have you come up for your letter?' she asked him.

'Yes. It suddenly struck me and I thought if it went to the cleaners . . .'

'Worse than that. I'm reading it.' She looked down. '"Moon like a watermelon." Where have I heard that before? Let's see what else there is. "Dancing on deck is one of the most romantic experiences. You, of course, had never known it in dull old England, and that's why . . ." ' She stopped reading and looked at him.

'Don't, Jane.' He was down on his knees beside her. Scott, looking puzzled, did the same. She found two pairs of eyes staring at her. John was pale and trembling.

'What can I say? I kept it because there's a poem in it I was interested in. She likes poetry.'

'Does she? Likes poetry? When did you become interested in poetry? Is that what you learned in the Army?' She bent her head to read more of the letter, but the words were dancing in front of her, and she swayed. John's arms went round her.

'I would have done anything to prevent this happening. I admit we were friends. Her husband was a doctor in India. We consoled each other.'

'I bet you did.' Her head was swimming. She tried to

161

focus on his face, but couldn't. 'Here, take it. It's yours.' She handed him the letter.

'Dr Maxwell! Dr Maxwell!' It was Caroline's voice, the new receptionist, outside in the corridor. 'Dr Moir wants to speak to you.'

'All right,' he called. 'I'll be down in a second.'

Scott had started to cry, bewildered with a situation he couldn't understand. He put his head in Jane's lap and she stroked it. 'There, there, Scott. We'll go out soon.' She looked up at John. 'If only I could cry I'd feel better. You'd better go down or he'll be up here too.'

'Jane, I can't tell you how sorry I am. I would do anything to undo this . . .'

'On you go. Go down. I'll see you at lunchtime.'

After he had gone she went into Scott's room and found him trying to put on his coat. 'Let Mummy help,' she said, 'and then we'll go out.' If only she could cry. What if the tears came when she was pushing him, and she met one of John's patients. They wouldn't expect her to be crying with the young doctor just home. She took Scott's hand, and together they negotiated the iron spiral staircase which took them to the garage, where she kept his go-chair. Scott had been so proud when he managed to go down alone, with her walking in front. She had made him into such a clever little boy for his daddy, who had paid her back by being unfaithful with someone called Ravella Choompal. No, she wasn't prepared to believe that they had only been friends. Hadn't Rachel set her wise about how men and women behaved nowadays. And hadn't she had the chance with Roger Mills and turned it down because of daddy? The word exploded in her brain and with it the tears came.

When she had strapped Scott in, they set off. She

thought of Stella Moir pushing an empty perambulator around the streets. Had she been more miserable than she felt at this moment? It wasn't difficult to subdue her tears. Her anger drowned them. She would never forgive him, never.

Pushing the go-chair along Main Street, she said good morning to several patients, feeling proud of her demeanour. So this is what it's like to be a betrayed woman, she thought. 'Yes, Mrs Paton, he got back last night. No, he hasn't changed.' She straightened her back as she walked on.

Fifteen

Boris arrived at ten o'clock, and after coffee together they set out. They had decided on Cahors for their shopping, because, as she said, Toulouse was for arrivals and departures, Gramon for everyday shopping and Cahors for window-shopping. She remembered many days doing just that, and marvelling at the choice compared with Gramon. Once there had been a small fair on in La Place Gambetta, and they had stood and watched the roundabouts for children, as if designed for fairy children, she had said, in admiration, and John had said that even in the smallest things the French showed their artistry. The whirling, gaudy-coloured coaches might have contained a prince and princess, and their entourage.

When Scott had been with them, he preferred to walk across the Roman Pont Valentré, and climb the steps in the look-out towers, from where one got a splendid view of the Lot, and the scenery around it. She and John had always preferred to penetrate the streets surrounding the Cathedrale St. Etienne, with their Middle-Ages flavour.

Cahors always seemed to have an air of the south, altough it was a long way from the coast, and the temperature, they swore, was distinctly hotter than Lab-

164

orie. They had agreed that it was because Laborie was near the Causse, and they sometimes felt a breath of wind from there, perfumed with herbs. The joints of lamb in Monsieur Gaillard's shop, which came from the Causse sheep, were scented also. 'Lamb from the Causse,' he would say proudly, holding out his pink offering so that they could smell the thyme.

When they got to Cahors it was lunchtime, so they sat in a street café and had a sandwich and a glass of beer, and watched the young people seated at tables around them. 'Like a small Paris,' Boris said.

'It's so evocative for me,' she said. 'I remember we came here the summer before John died.'

'You've never spoken about his death,' Boris said, leaning forward and putting his hand over hers.

'No, it was too difficult for me. I remember it was a dreary, wet winter with a snell wind blowing round corners. During that winter he had been coughing, he was subject to chesty colds, and I know I wasn't sympathetic enough. Our marriage had changed after he came back. There was a reason.' She thought of the woman's name, Ravella Choompal, but didn't say it.

'Go on,' Boris said. 'Father Anthony showed me the value of the confessional.'

'Yes, he's right. Well, he was in the habit of calling at a patient's house, Norman Cain, I could never understand why. I'm afraid I used to nag him about it, and one night there was a call from his wife, saying that Norman had taken ill. I told him he shouldn't go to them, it was three in the morning, and to wait, but he dressed himself, saying that the man was really ill, and he depended on him. He came back about five, having run this Norman Cain to the hospital – he'd had a heart attack. He subsequently died. From that night I noticed John got appreciably worse, he coughed a lot, and I blamed it on the night he had gone out to the Cains. In fact I was furious with everything, I had wanted us to leave the practice, and he had kept on putting it off.'

'If you're not in the best of health it's difficult to make decisions.'

'I realize that now. He got into a routine, but didn't complain. I hated the place, and had thought after the war we would move.' She couldn't tell him about the letter, and that she had realized for a long time how petty the incident had been.

'Death brings so many feelings with the grief; guilt, regret, and I've had to struggle with my conscience too,' Boris said. 'Looking back on our constant quarrelling I see that I was as much to blame as Hazel. We were incapable of meeting each other halfway. The knowledge that it's too late is difficult to accept. I've a feeling that being in Laborie helps. The people are less sophisticated, they are closer to nature, and you learn to live like them, to take life as it comes. Father Anthony says I should bring God into it, that I make it harder for myself.'

'I didn't have a Father Anthony. Perhaps that was my fault too. I didn't make friends easily.'

'I'd like to be your friend, Jane.' His eyes were full of pity. 'You must start by forgiving yourself. That's what I've been trying to do.' She felt the tears rolling down her cheeks.

'Oh, Boris,' she said, 'look what you've made me do. Crying in broad daylight.'

'That's good. Here . . .' He proffered a folded white handkerchief. 'That was washed and ironed by Mademoiselle Gregoire of the village.'

166

'One of your friends.' After she had wiped away the tears and finished her drink, they set off for the shop near Gambetta Square, but the furniture there looked as if designed for its windows, and they decided to wander down some of the back streets and search for something more individual. On the way, they passed a car show-room, and she said, 'Let's go in and buy my car.'

It was odd to say. 'I'm looking for a car, not a large one, for myself. I fancy a Peugeot.' She said this because it was a French marque, and why drive any other kind of car in France?

They listened to the young man extolling the virtues of the sleek grey model he showed them. '*Une voiture pour les dames,*' and it was good, she found, to say, '*C'est charmante,*' and, '*Je voudrais l'essayer.*'

The run was successful, and she negotiated the busy streets without any difficulty, after having had the dash-board explained to her. '*Madame, la conduit bien.*'

They arranged to have it delivered to her house the following day, after a thorough check-up, this, Boris, feeling he should take a part in the transaction, insisted upon, and she felt strangely excited when they left the shop. 'I feel quite peculiar,' she said. 'I've never bought a car before.'

'He looked at me suspiciously, when I didn't pay for it,' Boris said.

They had a drink to celebrate in a nearby café, and then proceeded on their rounds. Luck was with them. They came across a small furniture shop which looked promising, and went in.

'I shan't mind spending your money now,' she said to Boris. 'I think the French Provincial style here seems right for your house. It's more expensive than the shop at

La Place Gambetta, shall you mind?' He assured her he wouldn't.

They bought a dining-room suite, also chairs and a sofa for the lounge, with lots of small tables, and cushions, and lamps. Boris had ideas about the kind of lamps he wanted, and he also chose a desk for what he called his 'paper work'. 'That's what I missed in the caravan more than anything else,' he told her.

Driving back they were on that high only achieved by shopping in style. They told each other the regrets would come later.

He insisted on taking her to the Pont l'Isle, as a thank you for her help, and although she said the pleasure had been mutual, she was glad to accept. She felt they mustn't avoid talking about the accident, and dinner together would provide that opportunity.

'Do you feel you can settle in your house without Hazel?' she asked him.

'Yes, especially after today. It will occupy my mind arranging the furniture, and making the house into a home. I know she was beginning to entertain the idea of living there. We had fewer quarrels.' Jane wondered once again if they had been quarrelling that evening at the Mechoui when Hazel had offered to go with Jan.

'Just be content to know that she had come round to the idea of living in the house with you.'

'Yes. Do *you* still feel shaken by the accident?' he asked her.

'Yes. And no. I have been living in the past and it has brought me into the present. Like a kick-start. Do you know what I thought when I bought the car?'

'Tell me.'

'I said to myself, "I'm my own woman now."'

168

She saw his face change. 'But you'll continue to live here?'

'I'm not the urban type. You know Yeats' "Lake Isle of Innisfree"? That's me. Yes, I think so. I think I changed my mind in Cahors. I'll continue to stay here, but with frequent trips to London. I may drive from here, to fit in with my new image.'

'Don't get too ambitious. Remember what happened here.'

'I would never drive like Jan Graf.'

'Tell me, were the Grafs on the point of separating?'

'He did say that to me.'

'Was it because of you?'

'Definitely not. I'm not in the marrying mood.'

'Do you think that feeling will go on for ever?'

She met his eyes. 'I think so. I'm too old for that.' I had one lover, John, she thought. The best.

'Too old to take a lover?'

'It has its attractions. John was the one lover in my life. I was lucky, having that. I found out that there's a difference between attraction and love. I once met a man when I was young, and I didn't sleep with him, then when John came home, I found out he had been doing just that, with a woman. I felt affronted. That's a good Scots word. "Black affronted" my mother used to say. John knew I harboured a grudge. I think it took the backbone out of him, and out of our marriage. That was my fault, not his. I know because of me, he lost something, his enthusiasm, his decision. We disliked where we lived, the whole set-up, and instead of moving and making a new life, we went on punishing ourselves. We came to Laborie as an escape, when it got unbearable. He waited for me to say I forgave him, and I didn't do it. Too late now. I blame myself for his death.'

'You shouldn't go on punishing yourself, I told you that in Cahors.'

'Perhaps you'll be able to teach me that.'

'It's nice to look forward to us being neighbourly to each other, and then . . .'

'You'll teach me how to make amends?' She raised her glass to him, thinking if only it were John across the table from her, how different life would be.

He seemed to read her thoughts. 'Do you want to know what are the three most dangerous words in the English language?'

'Yes.'

'It was Father Anthony who accused me of using them. He's been a good friend to me . . .'

'Yes,' she said, thinking he's made a lot of friends through losing Hazel.

'One day he gave me an Edith Piaf CD.'

'"*Je regrette rien*"?'

'Right, first time. I'll pass it on to you. Or I'll play it when you come to see me.'

'I'll drive up.'

He smiled at her, as if he understood.

	DATE DUE		